6492

Do You
Remember
England?

Do You Remember England?

Derek Marlowe

THE VIKING PRESS

NEW YORK

TO SUKIE

Acknowledgments

The extract from *The Good Soldier,* by Ford Madox Ford, is taken from *The Bodley Head Ford Madox Ford,* Volume I, and is quoted by permission of The Bodley Head Ltd and David Higham Associates Ltd.

The lines from 'Missing Dates' are taken from *Collected Poems,* by William Empson, and are quoted by permission of the poet and Chatto and Windus Ltd, and Harcourt Brace Jovanovich, Inc.

The lines from 'Arabia,' by Walter de la Mare, are quoted by permission of The Society of Authors and the Literary Trustees of Walter de la Mare.

The lines from 'At Evening' from *Collected Poems of C. P. Cavafy,* translated by John Mavrogordato, are quoted by permission of the translator's Literary Estate, The Hogarth Press Ltd and Deborah Rogers Ltd.

Contents

We are all so afraid, we are all so alone, we all so need from the outside the assurance of our own worthiness.

So, for a time, if a passion comes to fruition, the man will get what he wants. He will get the moral support, the encouragement, the relief from the sense of loneliness, the assurance of his own worth. But these things pass away; inevitably they pass away as the shadows pass across sundials. It is sad, but it is so.

Ford Madox Ford: *The Good Soldier*

Part One

EMILY

One

No one quite knew why Dowson was at Stadshunt in the first place. He certainly hadn't been invited. He just appeared with two cousins who thought he belonged to someone else. He had arrived at the local station and they had assumed he was simply another guest of Benenden's. To be honest, the matter of his justification to be there had never arisen, for Dowson had said nothing, merely sitting in the front of the car next to the chauffeur gazing at the hedges. When the party finally arrived at Stadshunt, the other guests accepted him as being a friend of the cousins and dismissed it as that. It was only when he went for a walk before dinner that his presence there was questioned and by then it was too late. Benenden was much too embarrassed to ask him to leave and far too polite to ask him why he was there at all. Dowson simply became a guest and by the next day everyone decided that they never wanted to see him again in their life.

That was surprising really since he deliberately offended no one. He was simply himself, and God knows I wish I could enlarge on that. He was polite, presentable, allowed the hostess (Martha) to win at backgammon, and talked to the dogs when the occasion arose. Certainly his appearance was not orthodox as these things go—being rather too dark to be totally English, and having an accent that bore traces of London, rather than Oxford, but such idiosyncracies are not totally offensive. Especially at Stadshunt on a November evening.

Indeed Dowson, despite the enigma of his arrival, was a model guest. He drank only when offered, used the ashtrays discriminately, admired the Zoffany, told one rather charming anecdote and even went so far as to look at the family snapshot album without skipping a single page. He could play 'As Time Goes By' without vamping, admitted with endearing candour that he could neither ride a horse nor ski, remembered the children's names (but no one else's) and never once insisted on standing before the fireplace or filling in the blank spaces in the crossword. He praised the food (intolerable as it was), passed the port without hesitation and flattered each woman in turn with a style he could have acquired from Lothario. He was, in short, everything that a host could ask from a guest and, of course, everyone hated him.

When he left on the Sunday—the others had gone to visit Aunt Beth's rose garden (plus *bosquet*) and returned to find his room empty—there were no regrets. The silver was counted but there were no regrets. Dowson had come and gone and we hoped that that would be the last we would see of him. But we knew it wouldn't be, without foresight or pessimism. For he had stayed thirty-six hours, had glimpsed Hallam's wife only for a second (she was in a long silk dress, her hair loose, walking from the children's room, a book in hand) and I knew that nothing could ever be the same again. I cannot explain why. That is just the way it was.

There is now nothing more for me to add about that week-end or about Dowson, except for one small incident. Four of us were playing a game (Canasta) and Dowson was sitting in an armchair reading a book. I cannot say the name of the book, for it had lost its cover, but I remember studying him as the cards were shuffled. He was wearing a dark green velvet suit (not quite moss-green, somewhat darker) and was in profile. He was smoking a cigarette, and his eyes were lowered and at that moment (the fire, the lamp behind him), he appeared totally in his own entity, a portrait of a young poet in those long Edwardian summers, presenting a memory for those who would read his obituary after Ypres.

He appeared in truth, tragic and romantic—a coy cliché, I know, but I cannot attempt any more when one recalls what was to happen in those months ahead—and for a moment I was mesmerized. Perhaps others in the room felt the same sensation but I cannot be sure of that (there were indeed nine people counting Benenden and Hallam), though the Canasta game appeared to resume without hesitation. What I *can* be sure of is that Dowson suddenly looked up and gazed, not at me, but across the room, into the shadows and at no one and said quietly and without emphasis:

'Do you remember England?'

It appeared an absurd question—though it was said rhetorically, in statement. Then Dowson closed the book and carefully placed it on a table, got up and looked around at us all, one by one. He had remarkably blue eyes, very clear, translucent, irritating for being such an added advantage to his character, and then he turned sadly—I dwell on the last word, for his action was accompanied only by sadness, not for himself I am sure, but sadness that one sees in the faces of those who have lost something they have loved very deeply and know will never see again—turned and left the room.

The next day he never appeared for breakfast and by the afternoon, he had gone. A single pound note had been left under a figurine for the servants, and a single coin for an exercise book he had taken from the children's nursery. It's all madness, I know, but that was my first impression of Dowson and I wish more than anything that it had been my last. I can only correct one thing I have written. I stated that everyone hated him and it isn't true. Emily Hallam saw him only for a moment (she was staying at a neighbour's house and had passed by to visit the children before returning to a dance) and had seen him as he had left the drawing-room. No words were exchanged. He merely stopped on the stairs

19

and looked at her until she had entered her husband's room to prepare to leave.

When she left half an hour later, Emily saw him again. He was in his room, the door open, standing at the window, his right hand holding aside one of the chintz curtains (oleanders, pink and white). He was just standing staring out at the night, and the trees, not in observation exactly but more in a sense of nostalgia. There was no reason why Emily should have thought that, for he may have been merely day-dreaming. And yet he seemed totally unaware of her presence. Indeed to this day it is not clear why she did not simply glance in, see him and walk on. But it was an irrational weekend and the behaviour of everyone was unpredictable. He certainly did not belong to the room—at least not this kind of room, reproduced identically in every county in England. The warm bottle of Malvern water by the bedside, Morris wallpaper, and a train-journey biography of a whey-faced Queen (Alexandra, Mary, one or other of the Carolines) for the insomniac. He was just there. At the window. His back to her, a pensive anachronism. *Do you remember England?*

*　　*　　*

After that weekend, no one saw or heard of Dowson for almost two months, nor indeed was there any reason why they should, except for one occasion, totally without warning, in late January.

A party of us, including Hallam, had driven down to Lamberhurst in Kent to attend the wedding of Abel-Hardy's sister. None of us really liked the girl, or even her brother, but it was a pleasant journey and it had been rumoured that none other than Lucy Blakewell herself would be there unaccompanied—since her lover (a dress-designer of parochial repute) had reduced a decade of elegant posing to a hobble by breaking a leg in Gstaad, and consequently refused to appear in public until he could make his entrance wearing both shoes, size nine.

The wedding itself was memorable for its brevity, and afterwards some of the men gathered outside the church porch for a cigarette before moving on to the reception half a mile away. It was then that Dowson's name was mentioned, casually, for no apparent reason, by Abel-Hardy himself, who had been at Stadshunt, as he had been everywhere else recently, including Biarritz.

It was there that he had seen Dowson. At least, he had seen a young man in a white suit who looked remarkably like Dowson, walking with a middle-aged woman in a pink hat along the beach. They were just apparently walking side by side and he had watched them from his hotel.

'They did not seem to speak for a long time,' said Abel-Hardy, 'then they stopped and seemed to discuss something, very carefully, the woman looking up at him rather nervously, like two people debating a matter of utmost importance. As far as I could see, Dowson—if that's who it was—seemed totally apathetic to the woman, and yet without doubt it was he who was dictating the terms— God, that sounds suggestive now I say it, but I'm trying to be accurate. Biarritz had been bloody boring with those damn waves the height of a house, red flags all along the beach, so all I could do was sit on the terrace and stare and drink and wait for the Casino to fill up. But it certainly *looked* like Dowson. In a white suit, white hat, walking along the beach with this woman who must have been stinking rich, for she was staying on the same floor as I was.'

'Did you find out who she was?' someone asked.

'Well, I didn't play the detective, if that's what you mean, because frankly I couldn't give a sod about Dowson. But I was in the lobby the next day and one of the guests was being paged and it turned out to be this same woman. I had been watching her standing just near me, totally alone, and then when her name was called out she acknowledged it immediately and was handed a note. She opened it, read it and I remember she trembled and went as white as a sheet. Just like that. It was extraordinary. Don't know what the note said but she left the next day. All I could find out was that she wasn't English. That's all. Nothing else. I say— we'd better go. Everyone's gone.'

It wasn't until the reception was over that I had a chance to talk to Abel-Hardy again. He had spent almost the whole time supervising the champagne and the group photos (one quite charming one appeared in *Vogue* I believe. Forty of us on the lawn, shivering under a rather disdainful sycamore), and saving a nephew called Timothy from the ornamental pond. Bride and bridegroom left early for a honeymoon in New York (wedding night on a Boeing), while the wisest of us squatted on the floor before the television finishing off the smoked salmon, regretting the non-arrival of Lucy Blakewell who had probably spent *her* afternoon in bed with lover—plaster-cast, autographs and all.

Nobody inquired any more about Emily's absence—at least not to Hallam—leaving him alone on the knole sofa with two elderly ladies (aunts) who were under the coy impression that he had a fascination for preserves.

Then, at about seven o'clock, just as cars were turning in the driveway to return to London, I saw Abel-Hardy again. Alone. He was as drunk as I was, and so I offered him a lift in the back of my car.

'I've got stereo,' I said, 'and we could take some champagne with us and drink it on the way.'

'All right, but I'd like to know who that bastard was who said Lucy was going to be here. The cow.'

'Come on. Denbigh'll get us back to town in an hour. You could phone her up there and ask her.'

'If she's with Bridges, I'll break his other leg.'

'Get in. And bring some glasses.'

*   *   *

It was now dark, and by Sevenoaks we had finished the bottle, after spilling half of it over the carpet, and were sitting back silently, in a blissful haze, watching the passing woods, fields, clusters of cars outside roadside pubs, listening to a symphony by Vaughan Williams. 'The Pastoral'. Very English in that poignant, nostalgic way, evoking the same thought from both of us:

'I wonder if it *was* Dowson,' I said, turning towards Abel-Hardy. 'In Biarritz.'

I remember he didn't answer for a long time, not even moving but watching the black silhouettes of hills.

'When that woman left, he was still there. I saw him again two days later.'

'On the beach?'

'No. Not this time. He drove by me while I was walking along the promenade. He didn't see me but I saw him. Same suit, but no hat. That dark hair, very sun-tanned.'

'I didn't think he had a car.'

'Oh, it wasn't *his* car. I am sure of that. Italian thing. Bright orange. Must have cost a bomb.'

'Was he alone?'

A silence, then:

'No ... '

There was no elaboration, nor was it needed. The music had stopped and we were now approaching the suburbs of Croydon, both of us feeling very sober and pensive, not saying a word, almost resenting the intrusion of each other's company.

When we finally reached Sloane Street, Abel-Hardy merely said that he was just going to go straight to bed. Perhaps have a bath then an early bed.

'It was Dowson, you know. I'm sure of that. Damn pimp!'

'You can't be sure of that—' I said, but Abel-Hardy had slammed the door, and, as the car drove off, he was seen at the kerb, bending over, one hand supporting himself on a traffic sign as if he were about to be sick.

The next day Hallam received a parcel, postmarked *Milano*. It was a small rectangular envelope, about six inches by eight, that had been forwarded on to him, unopened, via Stadshunt. Inside was a red school exercise book (margin and lines) and before even opening the cover he knew who it was from. After all, it had already been paid for with a single coin.

Why he had sent it to him, I shall never know, as indeed I shall never know many things about Dowson. The first page was blank, then on the second page was written a verse from a poem in longhand—a poem in fact by William Empson. It is this:

> *From partial fires*
> *The waste remains, the waste remains and kills.*
> *It is the poems you have lost, the ills*
> *From missing dates, at which the heart expires.*
> *Slowly the poison the whole blood stream fills.*
> *The waste remains, the waste remains and kills.*

There was nothing more. The rest of the book was blank except for a child's drawing in blue crayon of a two-dimensional house on a hill and the single word

STADSHUNT

spelt out carefully underneath.

24

Two

At the age of sixteen, Emily was selected as one of Mr Cecil Beaton's Ten Most Beautiful Girls of 1956, and in consequence his photograph of her was reproduced in all the more fashionable newspapers and magazines of the day, as well as in one or two which were not. It shows the face of a young girl (I have a copy of it before me now), looking out of the frame at something that has introduced infinite sadness into her eyes and the corners of her mouth, as if the picture itself was merely a detail from a gigantic canvas (now lost) and she alone remains, a mere corner-angel witnessing some mythological tragedy she can share with no one.

There is beauty in the face certainly—the caption at least is justified—an English beauty that produces such paradoxes as the eyes themselves. They are not unfamiliar to the art-lover, for they are the eyes one sees created by the hand of Botticelli or the Pre-Raphaelites—large, oval, a heaviness on the upper lid, lashes encircling a remote and solitary secrecy (the image recurs) that solicits love and yet pity at the same time. They are unique eyes, granted to a rare few, and when I first saw them, in this very photograph, they appeared to be the eyes of a girl who was drowning, slowly, amid weeds. It is an absurd allusion, I realize, especially as I consider Ophelia outrageously melodramatic, but this impression persists, even to this day.

In the past decade, I have seen Emily many times, often in crowds, sitting opposite me at a table, collecting her children from school, but only rarely alone, unaware even of the presence of myself. Once in a Sussex garden, viewed from a window, standing very still in a lilac dress, the sun behind her, gazing at the first flowering of a clematis on the southern wall. Another, at an exhibition of Viennese art, sitting in the main hall of the Academy before one of the larger canvases (an Egon Schiele), sitting there quietly, almost as if she belonged in the room and could be found numbered and assessed in the catalogue, a priceless exhibit, *property of the owner*. The eyes had changed perhaps, older and even more beautiful, but the initial impression was still the same.

Her hair is long and fair, kept at shoulder length since the day she entered Society, but worn up, reminiscent of Juliette Recamier, at all special occasions and on the days she feels beautiful, and under a large flowered hat for weddings, picnics and the days when she feels plain. A long straight nose, encouraging profiles for the scrapbook, a wide full mouth, with teeth, alas, inherited from the aristocracy and more pertinently, her mother, and overcome only by vanity and a dentist (now dead) who used to have a surgery in Wigmore Street.

A long neck, thin body, small bottom, adequate legs (her worst feature) and a penchant, apparently, for weak health, though no one who met her would ever believe it. They only knew that she suffered from migraine, cooked with imagination, was a superb hostess, and that they would prefer to watch her playing Chopin at the piano rather than anyone else, including Chopin. Men fell in love with her from afar and wrote her poems which they sent to her, and women befriended her and talked about her to their friends. She was, in fact, to the outsider, everything a man would want for a wife—being beautiful, intelligent, rich and a daughter of one of the more liberal aristocratic families. She was every bachelor's dream and she spoilt it all, destroyed the fantasies, spoilt it all in one single gesture by marrying

Hallam two days after her seventeenth birthday just as the knights were entering the lists.

No man forgave Hallam for that and no man ever would, including myself. They just attended the wedding and went away. Then, when the babies were born (four in six years), prospective lovers who were obliged to become reluctant uncles, or worse, godfathers, attended christenings and went away again. A few who had loved her when she was young remained to become 'friends of the family'; others married women who resembled her and were moderately happy, while the others who loved her most never married at all. They are still single now, and if they are like me, always will be.

What is remarkable — and remember I am only an observer and will remain so — is that throughout all the years of her marriage, there was not a single rumour of Emily taking a lover, though it was known that she was unhappy throughout almost six of the eight years she lived with Hallam, in one place or another. Of course, there was always one self-proclaimed seducer who would hint at a liaison in Pitlochry or Montgomeryshire (photographers, novelists and Second Assistants are very prone to such things), but no one ever believed them, though they listened with interest. After all, she had every right to have an affair if that would make her happy, but deep down we were all too saturated with puritanical envy to hope that she would. The facts were plain enough and I see no reason to disguise them. Hallam had never earned a penny of his own since their honeymoon, had dabbled alphabetically in the various arts and failed in all, and had then turned, like the cat in that wretched adage, to drink. His success in marriage had secured him a series of mistresses from the remoter parts of Islington or Surrey, who considered it an achievement to replace Emily under her husband's body, even for an hour. And in a way, I suppose it was some kind of an achievement, for I believe Hallam always loved his wife and perhaps even adored her. That was his weakness, for he couldn't cope with her nor even understand her, and after a year he didn't even try.

They had married because she had fallen in love with him when she was fifteen, had lost her virginity to him at sixteen and never considered the possibility of anyone else. When she married him, he was as ambitious as Icarus. And when he fell, inevitably, seven years later, she blamed herself, as if she were the sun that had melted the wax. Perhaps she was, but it is too easy to see symbols in everything. All I know is that, for a while, she retired with her four children into the only possession she had left — a small house in Wiltshire. Hallam lived in London and continued, a rich drunk, visiting all the people who would still tolerate him. There was talk of divorce but from neither husband nor wife — she cared for her children, he cared for her money. It was a mere separation that might heal and sometimes, but very rarely, as at the Benendens', they would both be seen under the same roof.

On their first Christmas apart, a month after Stadshunt, Emily took the children to her parents' house in Cumberland — a large Georgian building that needed people and lights and presents under the tree. There was only the family there, including her two brothers, and they watched television and played games and went for walks with the dogs. Then, on New Year's Eve, they drove north across the border to a ceilidh; that was a traditional affair. Emily had always remembered this Hogmanay since she was a child and always cried at midnight as the piper appeared alone, on the darkened balcony of the house where they stayed. She loved Scotland for that, and cried this time inevitably, standing in the snow clutching her brother's arm and saying:

'I wish I was always this happy. Even for just another day.'

It was arranged that she should take a holiday alone, leaving the children with their grandparents. It was 'for the best', it was agreed. She needed to go away, preferably to the sun, away from England, away from all reminders of the past. And so, reluctant at first, she accepted. A cousin had a house on the island of Korčula, in the Adriatic, which she could have to herself and where they had friends nearby. It would be warmer there and very beautiful and she could take a diary and some books and could telephone home every other day.

In March, when it was spring, Emily went, tearfully as her brothers grinned moist-eyed at the airport and gave her presents and hugs and kisses and held up the children so that she could see them from the aeroplane window. She arrived in Korčula, via Dubrovnik, on the Thursday morning and found the small Renaissance town enchanting and sat in the square amid stone Venetian lions and pillars and wrote postcards to everyone she knew.

On the Friday, she began to feel homesick and discovered that all of her cousin's friends had left to sail south to Greece and wouldn't be back for at least a month. So she read two books on the balcony and went to bed early.

Then, on the Saturday, of course, she met Dowson.

$$* \quad * \quad *$$

It ought to belong to the mainland, and seen from the air it appears to wish it so. The coast of Yugoslavia reaches out towards it, an arm of a peninsula hovering over its eastern tip, fingers spread out to draw it in but frozen now, linked only by a mountainous shadow in late afternoon and a small ferry every four hours. The channel between is deep enough to allow boats from Athens and Dubrovnik to sail through on their way north to Split and Rijeka and west to Ancona, and some, I believe, even as far as Venice. They can be seen from the hills and the upper windows, large boats, white as the surf, moving slowly through waters the colour of hyacinth, and one expects glimpses of ladies with parasols and English nannies calling out to children in sailor-suits. An image of idle young men in blazers walking the deck with a maiden aunt and stewards in white and champagne and pretty girls with pale faces beneath hats of chrome yellow, sitting side by side, watching yet another island, and a copy of *Zuleika Dobson* waiting by the bedside table next to a letter postmarked Saffron Walden. It is not like that now, though the boats are the same, overcrowded with suitcases and bad-tempered tourists and a Fiat 500 on the upper deck; but the timelessness is there, and at dusk, with the lights and the temperate weather and the silhouettes of cypresses on the shore and the mountains beyond that, the beauty remains. It always has and it always will.

There is a legend that Odysseus visited Korčula and it may well be true. Certainly triremes from Rome lowered anchor in the bays, for broken temples can still be discovered in the olive groves (dedicated to Minerva, not to Pan) and a statue of Daphne, minus nose and index finger, lies face down beneath a laurel tree on the southern shore. In the thirteenth century, the Venetians visited the island and rebuilt the town of Korčula itself as it is today, a castellated port of atriums and gargoyles and narrow alleyways running down from its crest, presenting rectangles of sea to the tourist who has rested on the marble bench in its highest square, after visiting the Cathedral or perhaps buying a medallion in a corner shop.

'I read that there had been a plague here in the 16th Century,' Emily wrote to her mother in her first letter. I quote an extract only. 'And that everyone died, and those that didn't die ran away and left the town deserted. There are no red crosses on the doors now, but the town is deserted still. The tourists haven't yet arrived, and those Europeans who own the villas here are waiting for the summer. So I am alone. Not lonely, but solitary and trying hard not to think of the past. I have read two Agatha Christies – I am not ready for the Proust yet – and visited the museum.

'This morning I talked to the only person I have found who speaks English. An old man in the market place – very polite and very protective – who told me of the War. He was a partisan and very proud and showed me a house belonging to a Scotsman who is a great hero on the island because he helped liberate it from the Germans. The islanders call him *Il Generale* and say he is a kind man who has a very beautiful daughter, but neither of them were at home. The shutters were closed and the house looked empty and so I suppose they are waiting for the summer too.

'Other than the old man, I haven't talked to anyone yet, but I don't regret coming here. I miss the children terribly and you and everyone and have sent dozens of postcards and walked and walked when it wasn't too hot. But I don't regret anything. I never realized how tired I was and how much I needed *peace*. There are times when I feel I am the only person on the island and at night, except for the cicadas and a dog in a distant garden, I know that I am.'

There were many letters written on the second day (guide-book descriptions and exclamation marks to girl friends in Warwickshire and West London, drawings, rhymes and reminders to the children) as Emily sat either by the stone fountain (a gaping Medusa, rather badly carved) near the main steps, or later, when the sun was high, in the privacy of her own balcony overlooking rooftops of terracotta and the neighbouring islands, lounging in a blue canvas chair in the minimum of clothes, before falling asleep and waking to find it was dark. Three hours later, after eating a meal prepared by a housekeeper on the ground floor, she took a sleeping tablet (Mogadon) and didn't wake again until the Saturday morning was almost over.

*   *   *

Dowson had arrived by yacht from Italy. It was not his yacht. He was merely an invited guest who had befriended the owner in Rome.

The boat, certainly, was not beautiful, being almost one hundred and twenty feet in length; a two-master that had served duty for the American Navy in the Pacific, and had now been converted for both engine and sail and named after the Fijian word for peace. The owner had bought it when he was rich, after a succession of mediocre but successful motion-pictures in the early 'forties, and had vowed never to sell it. He had discovered that it was the only thing in the world he could rely on, not only because it obeyed him but also because it provided him with his only means of escape. Now that he was in his late fifties and forgotten (except by his creditors), he (Leith) had decided to tour the Mediterranean rather than the producers' offices, and had taken the minimum of crew, a young girl of fifteen called Melissa who shared his bed, three crates of vodka, and Dowson. 'We'll tour the islands, old sport,' Leith had said. 'We'll tour the islands until the bottles are empty,' and that is exactly what they did.

By the Straits of Messina, Leith's depression had lifted and he stood at the prow of the boat, standing beneath the rigging, in white flannels and yachting cap, paunchy but still handsome in the manner of the English officer he had played so many times in the past, when people queued to see his films and stopped him in the street and sent him billets-doux. But that was a generation ago and though the moustache remained and the archaic slang, there was little else. 'Once', he had told Dowson, sitting on deck beneath a starless sky, 'I would pick up a script and the description of the male lead would say: *Rodney, lean, handsome, cavalier, every woman's dream, every man's potential enemy.* That would be me. Today, if I ever receive a script, I know that it has been turned down by everyone else, and if I look for my part it isn't difficult; Rodney, a once-handsome man, now dissolute and a drunk, who dies on page thirty-two and who has less lines than those on my face.'

Leith had said this without self-pity, but as a statement, and then rarely talked about his past again, except to reminisce about his childhood in England. He never talked about the future either. He just grinned, poured another glass, then went below to sleep.

While they were in the Ionian Sea, he didn't appear for two days, though Melissa did, her eyes opaque, murmuring nonsense, her face painted like a Victorian puppet. At Corfu, Leith put on his only blazer, tied a cravat, took Dowson's arm and said: 'Come along, old chum. Let me show you the Greeks,' and then collapsed on the quay at the feet of a Bridge Party Excursion from Ohio. After that, they decided to sail north rather than south, where there would be less people, and on March 14th, after a stop at Dubrovnik, they docked eventually at Korčula.

The arrival of a boat was an event and Leith's yacht was no exception. The islanders could be seen lining up on the jetty from a distance of half a mile, as the immense two-master edged slowly towards the landing-stage. Dowson and Leith stood at the rail, the younger man in a white suit, the older in his yachting cap and flannels.

'Do you speak Serbo-Croat?'

'No,' said Dowson.

'Neither do I,' replied Leith, then smiled and added: 'Let's play the scene in English, then they can dub us in later.'

'I speak a little Greek,' Dowson said after a moment, as the palm trees and houses came into focus.

'Do you?' Leith exclaimed in amazement. 'I never knew anyone on God's earth spoke a *little* Greek.'

'My mother was Greek.'

'But I thought you were English.'

'My nationality is English but my mother was Greek.'

'Is she dead then, old sport?'

'Yes. Yes she is.'

They decided to eat immediately. At least Dowson decided, since Leith ate little and Melissa was never in any condition to decide anything. A restaurant was found at the foot of the old town that resembled a hundred other Mediterranean restaurants and one was grateful for that. It was called the *Planjak*: tables set out on the cobblestones, a charcoal stove, a canopy of vines to shade the customers from the sun and where lanterns were hung at night. It was small and inviting and half empty and the three visitors sat at a corner table, Dowson with his back to the other customers, a cigarette in one hand gazing out pensively at a cat sleeping on a nearby window-sill.

'Do you think they speak English?' Leith inquired and Dowson looked at him and smiled and looked away.

'I mean, they must understand the word vino, wouldn't you say?' Leith continued, rather helplessly, and looked at Melissa, who was carefully folding a leaf into the shape of a star which she would wear in her hair.

A menu was placed before them and Dowson ordered a bottle of local wine, speaking in a mixture of Greek and Italian, and a litre of *posip* was placed before them. They drank it slowly as if they were strangers, which in truth they were. Three people who had met by chance in the Piazza Navona and who were now sitting on an island four weeks later, self-consciously avoiding each other's eyes, suddenly aware that they were all outsiders, not only to the world but also to each other. Behind Dowson, a woman in a straw hat and yellow dress sat down and opened a paperback novel, her chair-back resting against his.

'It's translated into English,' Leith discovered finally, pointing at the menu. 'English and German. *German!* Bloody thick-skinned of them, wouldn't you say? Coming back here with their Volkswagens and their copies of *Stern* to see what they almost had.'

'Did you fight the Germans?' Melissa asked, her voice American, nasal and bored.

'Single-handed, sweetheart,' replied Leith deadpan and held up the empty bottle to the waiter, but he was already attending to the woman behind Dowson.

She was unsure and had wanted to order one of the national dishes but they had not been explained, nor could the waiter understand. Finally, Dowson turned round, rested his hand on the waiter's arm and said quietly:

'Raznjici, per favore, per la signora,' and then turned to the woman. 'It's a kebab, probably with lamb. It is what I will choose.'

Emily nodded and looked away.

'You may join us at our table if you wish,' Dowson added, pointing to an empty chair.

'No, thank you.'

'Of course. You are waiting for your husband.'

'No. I am alone here,' replied Emily quickly, without forethought and yet without invitation, for it was a phrase she had just written in her journal two hours before. She was alone in Korčula, a thousand miles from anyone she loved or who loved her and it was simply the realization of that.

'What a coincidence,' Dowson said, gazing at the book she held in her hand, then glancing up at her.

'But you are with friends,' Emily replied and turned the book face down. It was *Le Grand Meaulnes*. Unread.

'A coincidence that we should meet again—here of all places. Or have you forgotten that we saw each other before?'

Emily looked at him, looked at Dowson a few inches away from her, not at his eyes, but at his nose, his mouth, his hair. There was a pause, then she stood up and said: 'No. I don't remember at all. I'm sorry ... ' and picked up her book and left the restaurant. Dowson watched her till she had crossed the square towards the steps. A last glimpse of saffron, a hesitation, then she was gone.

'Hard luck, old chum,' he heard Leith say. 'That approach doesn't seem to work any more. I think I killed it long ago.'

Dowson gave a brief smile and nodded and turned back towards the table. Melissa was yawning.

'It must have been somebody else,' he said and as far as Dowson was concerned that was the end of it. After all, tomorrow they would be sailing to Venice, which he had never seen. It had been arranged and there seemed, of course, no reason to change it.

Three

They spent the evening on the boat after visiting part of the town in a half-hearted gesture of sightseeing, though Dowson preferred to wander the streets alone for an hour before returning to join the others in the main cabin. He found Leith in good humour, demonstrating the art of sword-fighting with a walking-stick to Melissa, who sat cross-legged on the floor, nodding to herself. Dowson watched the performance for a while until the actor was exhausted.

'I used to be better than this,' sighed Leith leaning against a table. 'Once I was champion of Beverly Hills.'

'I believe it,' said Dowson, 'I remember seeing you in *Robin Hood.*'

Melissa looked up at Leith in blank amazement and asked: 'Who did you play in *Robin Hood*?'

'Robin bloody Hood, of course. Who the hell did you think I played? Maid Marian?'

'I just don't remember you in *Robin Hood*, that's all. I saw it on TV and I just don't remember you.'

'There have been dozens of Robin Hoods, sweetheart. Dozens.'

'Yours was the best,' said Dowson quietly.

Leith looked at him shyly, a slight embarrassment and didn't reply for a moment, then said:

'Let's go on deck. It's stifling in here.'

The two men walked to the cabin steps, then Leith stopped and looked back at Melissa who was gazing at him, frowning, as if dry-running a statement of profound importance.

'Don't say anything,' he warned. 'Don't say anything at all. Just go to bed.'

'But it's only nine o'clock.'

'I know. Don't wait up.'

Leith then took a bottle from the table and walked up to the deck.

'I could have gone to Morocco,' the girl said to no one in particular as Dowson closed the door, leaving her alone.

Dowson drank only one glass of vodka as a token gesture to his companion as they both sat on the deck, the walls of the town behind them, gazing across at the lights on the mainland. In the night, an illuminated cross on a mountain church seemed to hover in the sky, as perhaps was the intention, but the effect was grotesque and pretentious, the only disturbing image in the tranquility of the view.

'You don't talk much about yourself, old sport,' said Leith casually.

'Neither do you,' answered Dowson.

'Nothing worse than an actor talking about himself. Besides, if I kept a scrapbook, which I don't, it would only be filled with stories of court cases and divorces, and no one, least of all myself, ought to be reminded of those. I've been fodder for the third-rate comedian for too long. Want a cheap laugh? Tell a story about Leith. It used to hurt me once, would you believe? But now ... '

Dowson glanced across at Leith's profile in the darkness, the Abe Lincoln nose (the cartoonist's delight), the thin moustache and the hint of a weak chin. The sun-tan had covered the smaller lines and the veins but it was the face of an old man, tired, disillusioned and ultimately very, very bored.

'Do you know where I would like to be now?' Leith said.

'No. Where would you like to be now?'

'England, old sport. I haven't been there for years and

when I did it was raining. But that's where we should be. Back in dear old Blighty ... '

Dowson smiled and didn't reply for a long while, gazing at the sky. From the cabin he could hear Melissa attempting to tune a transistor radio from language to language to music. Finally, he said very quietly, almost as if he were thinking out loud:

'During the War, we stayed in a village in Yorkshire. My mother and myself. It was a small village with a church and a manor and a farm and nothing else. There must have been houses there, but I can't remember them. I can't even remember the people, only the countryside. Like a dream where only you exist. And like a dream, there was a time-lessness and a happiness that I've never experienced since. It sounds over-nostalgic, and I know that over the years I've turned it into a Romantic illusion, but then I don't want the memory to change. To me, that is *my* England. Unreal, perhaps, but there's a security. In the memory. And if I ever returned – I mean, return to live, it'll be to *that* England ... '

He paused, considering what he had said, then shrugged:

'Anyway, it probably doesn't exist any more. And perhaps it never did. But then as long as we are not there, we can't be disillusioned. Can we?'

There was no answer and Dowson turned and looked at Leith. For a moment it seemed as if the actor had died, without warning, the cigarette in his left hand neglected, but he was merely submitting without a struggle to the alcoholic trance with which he was now so intimate. In time, his eyes would close and he would fall asleep and Dowson would help him to his cabin before the air grew too cold. But at the moment, the evening was still temperate and the sky was cloudless.

Dowson remained on deck for a further two hours, oblivious of the curiosity seekers who were staring at the boat from the quayside. The Mediterranean had rarely held any fascination for him, and so he treated it and the people with apathy, including the Greeks. Instead he chose to play the role of the voluntary exile, and consequently, as he described later, he could, on that particular evening, have been anywhere.

* * *

'It *is* Mrs Hallam, isn't it?' Dowson said.

We are in the market-place the next morning. A concrete bull-ring of stalls, built on the outside of the town so that the cars can park. A collage of palm-trees, vegetables and fruit (new potatoes, zucchini, spring onions), carvings from Turkey, carpets, hawkers, a crescendo of bartering. Dowson is in white with a pale yellow shirt. Emily in watchet blue, a sleeveless cotton dress, blonde hair under hat, turning, the sun dazzling her eyes, one hand rising to her face. The steps to the old town to our left, the sea to our right. It is not yet hot enough to swim but the forecast is reliable.

'You need not reply,' continued Dowson, seeing the hesitation in Emily's face. 'I know that sometimes the last person one wants to meet abroad is someone from England. But since you obviously didn't remember me yesterday, I don't want you to think that it was my intention to embarrass you.'

'You didn't embarrass me,' Emily replied, simply and without emphasis.

Dowson smiled.

'Then you *are* Mrs Hallam?'

'Yes ... '

'We met at Stadshunt. At least I saw you there for a brief instant. You were wearing a white dress and your hair was loose and not pinned up as it is now —'

'Yes. I remember. I was going to a dance and had called in to see the children.'

A pause. Emily looked away and watched two women bargaining at a nearby stall, their voices counterpointing each other in volume and intensity, then she heard Dowson say:

'My money is on the woman on the left. She seems more determined. That jawline ... '

Emily smiled and nodded but didn't look at the young man next to her. She suddenly felt very nervous and fragile, unable to move. She wondered if he had been waiting for her, planning the encounter; but then all of Korčula came to the market-place at this time of the day. He had come to buy provisions like everyone else, and the meeting itself was simply an accident. That was all.

'My name is Christopher Dowson. It is not English, I know, to introduce oneself, but it makes it less formal. Especially here.'

They shook hands politely, Emily removing her hand from his first, then moved away.

'I must buy some food for lunch. My housekeeper is not well so I volunteered. We talk in gestures like shadow puppets but I think she understood.'

'Then perhaps I can be of assistance. As you can see, it needs more than gestures to buy anything here.'

'It is not necessary—'

'Perhaps not, for I am sure the shopkeepers would give you the food for nothing. But I have to buy supplies for the boat and you could be of great assistance.'

'In what way?' asked Emily, startled.

'I have no eye for quality,' Dowson replied, gesturing to a table of courgettes. 'They all look the same to me. That one equals that one to my untrained eye, and yet these women select each vegetable, each fruit with the calculation of a chess-player.'

Emily suddenly laughed and looked up at Dowson and found to her surprise that he was blushing slightly and was about to say something to deflect his embarrassment when an Arab boy, no more than fourteen, in fez and burnous, approached grinning and held up an embroidered bag with fringes to Emily. With the merest movement, hardly perceptible, she shook her head, then said no and smiled and the boy lifted his shoulders in a theatrical shrug and walked a few paces away and stopped and looked at them both.

'Now I see that you don't need me at all,' said Dowson, looking at her. 'It would have taken me ten minutes to get rid of him and I would probably have lost my temper.' Then he smiled shyly and turned away:

'Goodbye, Mrs Hallam. It was pleasant to meet you again.'

Before Emily could react he was gone, and she suddenly found that the market-place was filled with people who were jostling her and thrusting out hands holding objects for her to buy, and she was aware for the first time of the screaming and the begging and, worst of all, of the alien voices.

*   *   *

When Dowson returned later to the landing-stage, the yacht was gone. For a moment he thought he might have lost his way and arrived at the wrong quay, and was just about to walk away when a man approached him who had obviously been waiting for him.

'Signor Dowson?'

Dowson looked at him then nodded. The man smiled and handed him a sealed envelope.

'I am to give you this and you are to give me one hundred dinari.'

It was a note, written in pencil, from Leith:

'Old Sport: Change of plans. The zombie wants to visit the local islands à deux, since she's heard about nude swimming. Can't resist

42

*at my age and you're too much competition for my vanity. Be back
soon. L.*

P.S. Give the wog 50.'

* * *

Dowson ate lunch at the *Planjak*, as before, after buying
a paper-tissue facsimile of *The Times* (two days old) from a
newsagent nearby. He had read everything, including a
rather pedantic keepsake on the Coal Industry, when Emily
arrived, dressed as she was earlier, but with her hair now
unpinned and without a hat.

'Mr Dowson,' she said quickly, approaching his table. 'I
did not mean to offend you this morning. If I did, I am sorry.'

Slowly, Dowson raised his head and looked up at her,
studying her across the table very carefully and yet without
impertinence, as if she were a statue by Cellini he had discovered in a neighbour's back-yard. His appraisal was not
reserved for the rare beauty alone but more for the fact that
it was there in the first place.

He noticed details: a small scar the shape of a scimitar on
her left arm, the wedding ring, another ring consisting of
diamonds and sapphires, the hands themselves, unlined, as
if they had been preserved in gloves since she was a child.
He noticed the pattern on the dress (fuchsias on a field of
blue), her neck, the suggestion of a crease on her chin, a
constellation of summer freckles on her nose, and then, of
course, the eyes themselves, looking down at him, then
glancing away but only for a moment. He noticed also the
bag she clutched in front of her. It was the embroidered one
with fringes that she must have eventually bought from the
Arab boy, but he made no comment either by expression or
by word. Dowson merely asked Emily to sit down and join
him for coffee which he had just ordered.

And she did.

* * *

'There is an actual case history of a girl of sixteen who had never seen her own face in her life. She believed herself a vegetable and lived in a darkness and yet on the wall of her room in the asylum was a photograph of herself, blurred but recognizable, standing with three companions. But to the girl, the face was that of a stranger, and she was unaware that it was herself, until one day a mirror was left in her room. It took her four days apparently to look into it, considering it an enemy; and then on the fifth day she was found sobbing in a corner clutching the mutilated photograph in her hand.

I have no idea why I have quoted this story on this blissful day in the Adriatic, except that it has entered my mind and I cannot get rid of it unless I write it down. It is all I will write today. I am in no mood any more for diaries.'

* * *

Dowson and Emily did not meet for twenty-four hours after that encounter in the restaurant. They had talked for an hour, obliquely, then arranged to meet the next day in order to visit the *Moreska*, a local attraction they had been urged to see by the head waiter, who believed them both to be husband and wife and called them *Signor* and *Signora* and pampered them with free liqueurs.

Leith didn't return that evening, so Dowson stayed at a local hotel and hated it. In the morning, he walked down to the harbour once more and the yacht still wasn't there, nor was it in sight, so he took the precaution of buying another shirt, toothbrush, toothpaste and underclothes (his belongings now moored anywhere within a radius of fifty miles) and submitted to a shave from the hotel barber. In cash he had less than ten pounds and decided to charge the bill for his room to Leith, whenever he might return.

At noon, while waiting for Emily to arrive at the restaurant, he saw the Arab boy again. He was reminded of his father, who had spent almost twenty years of his life in the deserts of Egypt and Arabia, volunteering for the Royal Signals in 1925 when the dole queues began to line up on the corners of the streets. There were sepia photographs of him in a small black album, rarely opened, showing a young handsome man, moustached and prematurely balding, standing in shorts and pith helmet by the waters of the Nile or outside the old Shepheard's Hotel in Cairo. One of Dowson's mother too, a month before she was married in Alexandria and taken in Alexandria itself. Under the photograph — a wistful young girl in a cloche hat, posing on a balcony, deep shadows from an afternoon sun, shutters — his mother had written in white ink four lines by Cavafy in Greek. Translated they are:

> I went out sadly on to the balcony —
> Went out to change my thoughts if only by seeing
> A little of the city I loved,
> A little movement in the streets and shops.

Dowson had told Emily the previous day that as he loved England, so his mother had loved Greece, though she was an exile, outlawed by one junta in the 'twenties and destroyed by another in the 'sixties. She had returned to her native country only once after leaving as a child, returning alone to discover if any of her relations were still alive and if they remembered her. She never returned to England, dying in the house in which she was born, on another island in the Mediterranean from where her son was now, at the age of forty-nine. It was suggested that she had committed suicide, but there was no proof. The officials simply buried her on Leros next to her mother and her grandmother.

When Emily asked Dowson if he had ever visited the grave, he had shaken his head and replied that he would rather remember his mother when she was young and alive (for that could never change) than see the place where she was dead.

*   *   *

The *Moreska* was a battle between kings performed in a courtyard in the town of Korčula itself. A story of rivalry over the love of a captured princess (Bula) in which monarchs (black and red) meet, boast, prance then finally enact a war of such danger and skill that blood is often drawn. It is said that the youths of the island train for years to qualify to fight in the pageant, and certainly the sword-fighting alone is enough to convince the visitor that it could surely happen only once in a generation. And yet it is performed twice a week in high summer by the same cast, casualties (one is assured) are minimal, and Good always triumphs over Evil, despite the precedents. Bula returns finally to the honoured victor in scarlet, her face pale, a garland of flowers in her hair, murmuring, 'My love, my dear sweet love,' and raises her veil to be kissed.

Emily and Dowson were not disappointed. They sat side by side within a portico, now and again glancing at a translation in their hand, and did not speak until the *Moreska* was over and the courtyard was empty.

They had in fact spoken hardly at all that day, since they met, and to the casual observer they appeared to be shy of each other, taking care not to touch each other, nervous of even a sleeve brushing accidentally against an arm. They certainly could not be taken to be brother and sister; their very appearance belied that. She fair, in white, with almost a winter skin, at times remote, smiling politely, frail. A person from England. While her companion, whose skin had now darkened rapidly under the sun, seemed to be anything but English: a young Greek, despite the blue eyes, as part of the Adriatic as the island itself.

If not related—and remember one is watching them

unobserved – then not lovers either. That indeed is evident, for the woman's eyes betray too much. There is affection there, a deceptive shyness and even a trace of guilt, but that is all as yet. From the young man, we can discover nothing. Basic emotions of pain, anger and excitement could perhaps be registered on that face, but little else. Not because it is insensitive (quite the contrary) but because the owner has chosen the mask he presents to the world, and only rarely, seeing him suddenly unawares, does one detect the true character underneath. I myself saw it that evening at Stadshunt, and described it as tragic and romantic, producing perhaps a sympathy in the reader towards Dowson that may well be deceptive. I am aware of that, and though I know the events that will follow all too soon, the phrase remains. At the moment, however, the two people who are crossing the courtyard side by side (a cardboard crown lies abandoned under a bench) are simply friends. Not quite at ease in each other's company, but friends nevertheless. That, at least, they both know.

'Let us go to the harbour,' Dowson said. 'Perhaps the yacht has returned.'

'It is not your yacht is it?'

'No,' Dowson smiled, 'nor would I want it to be.'

'Why?' Emily asked. 'Do you not like boats? I thought everyone from England or Greece liked boats. The English preferring the small, the Greeks the large.'

'That may be true, but the point is I cannot swim,' and Dowson laughed, encouraging Emily to touch his arm for a moment, smiling, then move away so that the action was hardly noticed.

'And yet,' Emily said, 'you travel in someone else's boat. The risk surely is the same.'

'When you see this yacht you will realize that only a torpedo could sink it, and they, I believe, are rare nowadays.'

'Or an iceberg. Like the *Titanic*.'

'That I must admit I never considered. Remind me to tell Leith to avoid Greenland on our way back to Italy.'

Emily looked at Dowson, pensive for a moment, then asked:

'The man at your table when we first saw each other here. Was that Leith?'

'Yes. Did you not recognize him? He'd be very upset.'

'Then he *is* the actor who used to be in all those pirate films? The waiter was right.'

'Yes, he was.'

'And I thought he was dead.'

'No. He's not dead. He's just dying.'

Dowson said this quite simply, though by the very fact of stating it, it appeared flippant, almost callous.

'I'm sorry,' he said quickly. 'I didn't mean that to sound—'

'It's all right,' Emily interrupted immediately. 'We must not keep apologizing to each other for everything we say. Let us just go and see if the boat has returned.'

Dowson nodded and they walked out of the courtyard into a square and towards the steps that descended beneath the main gate of the old town to the port. Already they could see the main steamer from Rijeka waiting beyond the palm trees along the waterfront.

'Leith would like you very much,' Dowson said looking across at her as they walked. Emily, aware of the compliment (the first, though indirect), smiled:

'I hear he likes *all* women. Isn't that his reputation?'

'His reputation, yes. But he will like you nevertheless.'

'And will I like him?'

Dowson didn't answer, not having considered the situation, then replied:

'Yes. *I* do.'

A silence. They walked on. The conversation didn't end there but it returned, as if by mutual consent, to generalizations: the island, the weather, the *Moreska*. *England*. They never discussed each other's private lives other than the common experience of schooldays (far different) and the War, nor did they ever question why either of them was in Korčula in the first place. Once, Emily had seen a wooden toy in a shop and had said spontaneously that she must buy it for Victoria, but that was the only time anything relating to her marriage was mentioned and Dowson never inquired. All he knew was that she was a married woman with four children, and from the aristocracy, a class for which he felt (unlike the celebrities who flaunted their working-class background as if it were an anointed stigma) neither admiration nor antipathy.

Dowson also knew that he no longer wanted to leave Korčula as long as Emily was there, even if they never spoke to each other again. He had no dreams, no aspirations towards their relationship, for even to consider them seemed insane. He just wanted to stay at the perimeter of her existence and admitted finally to himself as they approached the harbour, that he wouldn't care if Leith *never* returned.

'Is that his boat?' said Emily, pointing along the quay.

Dowson turned slowly and looked at the two-master moored twenty yards away, the sound of a transistor radio from below deck. Then he said finally:

'No. Leith's boat is bigger and painted white.'

'Then he hasn't returned?'

Dowson looked around the harbour and shook his head:

'No, not yet. But he will.'

*   *   *

Emily was pleased that Leith was still away from Korčula. She would not admit it, even to her diary, but she knew she preferred to be with Dowson alone.

That evening, for an hour, while waiting for him to arrive (they had agreed to have dinner at a lobster restaurant outside of town), she tried to rationalize the past two days. Certainly she knew that her loneliness had contributed to her agreement to meet Dowson again, as well as the romance of the island itself, but she had always considered herself a practical woman at heart, quite capable of resisting any chance of an affair, no matter what the mood or who the person was. She was, after all, still married, as well as being a mother, and she had not disguised the fact. She was also twenty-seven years old, an age that ought not to encourage casual flirtations.

And yet Dowson had never behaved in any way improperly, even for a moment, and had never attempted to advance their relationship further than a polite acquaintanceship. For all she knew he may himself be married (he wasn't) or at least be in love with someone in England and was simply bored. It was possible that he had arrived in Korčula by chance, been abandoned temporarily by his friends and was bored. There were no other English people there, and he had taken the opportunity to pass the time with her, rather than remain alone. There could be nothing more than that, and in a way, Emily was relieved. She need fear nothing, for if the gossip she had heard in England was true (and gossip there was), Dowson was a gigolo without scruples who would have attempted to take advantage of the situation without hesitation. But he had not. Either the gossip was wrong or Dowson found no attraction in her whatsoever. Nevertheless, Emily could not deny that she was flattered.

As she bathed and dressed, she was aware, with almost adolescent nervousness, that this was the first occasion she was waiting for a man to call, to take her out alone, since she had met Hallam. There had been opportunities and there had been proposals, but she had always found an escape in the excuse that she was a married woman, no matter how unhappy the contract had become.

Even when she finally accepted the fact that her husband had lovers, she still resisted the attentions of other men. In part, this was because all the men were friends of friends in the ever-increasing circles of society in which she moved, and in part, it was fear. But now, at the moment, she was not in England, and Dowson was an outsider, whom even six months ago no one in that vast arena around her knew even existed. When Leith returned he would leave, and until then they would be unobserved. There was, she convinced herself, security in that.

By eight o'clock, she had put on and taken off three different dresses. She had carefully and painstakingly pinned her hair up, then at the last moment decided to wear it loose, and spent a further ten minutes brushing it. She regretted not having brought another suitcase of clothes, had placed a photograph of her children (taken in Kensington Gardens) into a drawer, then put it back on the table. She tidied the small living-room, washed a coffee cup found neglected on the balcony, and then just as she was searching her bedroom for cigarettes, she caught a reflection of herself in the wall-mirror and stopped, as if frozen on film, and looked at herself, then slowly sat on the edge of the bed, gasping for breath, and didn't move.

When Dowson arrived forty minutes later, there was no answer. He walked around the side of the building and looked up at the windows, saw there were no lights on, checked the number and street, then knocked on the front door again. Finally the housekeeper appeared from a back room (a television could be heard, grannie with arthritis) and looked at Dowson with a mixture of puzzlement and irritation.

'È la Signora Hallam qui?'

The housekeeper hesitated then glanced up at the darkened stairway behind her, shook her head, then looked at Dowson suspiciously and shook her head again more emphatically and closed the door.

From behind the half-closed shutters above, Emily watched, her face pale, and saw Dowson walk away, stop, look at the house, then suddenly write a message on a piece of paper and walk back towards the house. She retreated quickly into the centre of the room, holding her breath, listening until she heard his footsteps walk away again and then there was silence.

Slowly she opened the living-room door and stared down the stairs at the white piece of paper that was now lying on the flagstones. For a moment she didn't move, then walked down the stairs, feeling absurd and foolish as if she were a child creeping out of the dormitory after hours, reached the note and picked it up.

She read it, standing in the half-light, a page ripped from a pocket-diary containing four days in a season that had not yet arrived. It said simply:

Impossible to find transport to the lobster restaurant, so I am dining at the Planjak. *I am there now. Your house was in darkness so I went away.*

*　　*　　*

It took an hour for Emily to abandon her pride sufficiently to leave the house, and when she did she had to restrain herself from hurrying down the steps towards the restaurant. She anticipated the moment when she would see Dowson sitting alone at a table and had rehearsed what she would say. She had made her decision and looked forward to seeing him and talking to him with an eagerness she thought she had abandoned many years ago, placed in a drawer together with her first evening-dress and matching shoes.

When she arrived at the *Planjak* he was there of course,

but he was not alone and by the time she saw him, it was too late. He appeared to be surrounded by dozens of people at a large table, laughing and talking in Italian, voices ricocheting across the square, acknowledged her arrival with only the briefest glance, and then didn't talk to her for an hour, except to say, 'I have already ordered for you. Sit down here,' and turned back to the other people as if her presence was nothing less than superfluous. And, in truth, it was.

She tried to join in, to belong to the party, but she spoke no Italian and the visiting tourists spoke no English. One or two smiled at her, and offered her wine and attempted a conversation but gave up with a sympathetic shrug and clustered around Dowson. In time, she was simply ignored. After ten minutes, Emily attempted to leave but found herself hemmed in, so that the very act of moving embarrassed her. She felt angry and humiliated, for the attention she expected (and indeed was used to) was being denied her, and yet she admitted reluctantly that it was, despite everything, her own fault. Her husband, at various times in their marriage, had called her spoilt, stubborn and selfish, and true or not, she now realized that evening that she had demonstrated all three characteristics, and so, as if in penance, she stayed. After half an hour, she wanted to be nowhere else.

Emily sat and stared at Dowson, watching him across the glasses and the bottles, his face highlighted by a lantern to his left. He seemed to be totally at ease, laughing, hugging the arm of an old woman as she giggled at an anecdote, charming all those around him so that they jostled eagerly, men and women alike, to be near him and draw his attention. This image of Dowson she was never to forget, and as the months passed she realized how rare in fact it was. It set, regrettably, few precedents.

But now it was the first time she had seen him so completely happy, looking at each person in turn (except herself) and favouring all. And when three of the younger Italians began to sing, accompanied by a guitar, he didn't join in but encouraged them, smiling, filling their glasses and Emily became aware of the *frisson* of being within his company. It sounds melodramatic, I realize, but such things often are, and the words are hers as she described them much later. I myself can portray the scene in no other way; I am incapable of it and it is useless to try. Emily was just suddenly aware that she was happy, that she had not been really conscious of happiness for years, and she had almost missed it, almost thrown it away, finding excuses in tired morals and ancient vows, and the sudden thought of that made her close her eyes for a moment, her skin cold, trembling. When she opened them, Dowson was smiling and looking at her for the first time since she had arrived. Then he sat down beside her and rested his hand gently on her arm and said:

'When you are ready, Emily, we will go. The game is over.'

* * *

A light shimmering, converging within itself, merging within another light the shape of a discus and moving together then separating, and overlapping in the furthest corner of the ceiling, then breaking into pieces as the waves beneath the balcony recede into the shadow. The laughter of children, murmurs, shouts, another sound, at first unrecognizable to Emily, then identifying itself as a lawn-mower, hesitating as it reaches a border perhaps, then returning to the parallel. Other sounds: a door closing suddenly on the hotel floor above, a voice raised to call a greeting, a telephone ringing, a car promoting its gears on a steep hill in the distance. Images. Moods, the awakening, the tranquillity of early morning and the sun above it all moving towards her eyeline, bisecting the room and casting a ladder of shadows from the shutter on to the carpet. Curtains disturbed gently, a chair with her dress on its lap, a single shoe, a print (sepia) framed on the opposite wall, sheep wandering amid ruins. Desk, the edge of the bed, her hand, palm up, lying on the sheet, a telephone ringing. Motionless, a gentle trembling gilding the edge of her skin, a chasm of peace spread out before her as if seen from above. The day presents itself with the gift of minutes, hours, to be shared together, a renaissance of experiences she blissfully anticipates. Reborn, the memory ceases beyond the past twelve hours; she drifts, floats, her eyes close and she turns, her hair embroidering the pillow, the sheet easing away to expose her back (white as copy-paper, a charcoal sketch of shadows) turns across the bed as the telephone stops ringing. He picks up the receiver as she moves her mouth towards his shoulder and hears:

'Hallo, old sport —'

The mosaic splinters.

' — I'm back.'

Four

Emily liked Leith immediately. Not because he was Dowson's friend nor because he flattered her with good manners, but simply because he accepted the fact of her and Dowson together without question, was aware of her immediate shyness and was considerate, and she was grateful for that.

They had met him in the bar of the hotel easing himself into the day with a large Bloody Mary, and he had smiled at her and taken her hand reassuringly and had put his arm around Dowson's shoulder.

'Oh ... ' he said, looking at them, after Emily had been introduced, 'you would never believe how good it is to see you both. You're a vision. There are no other words for it,' then he turned away embarrassed, finished the drink and ordered another.

Dowson and Emily sat down next to him in silence, not looking at him nor at each other, but out across the room towards the windows and the sea beyond. A waiter approached, they ordered coffee for themselves, then remained, sharing their own entity, memories of the past night. 'A warm serenity,' she described to me later, and quoted a verse by Frances Horovitz she had written down and left in his room for him to read when he was alone. She was aware of the patterns of love, intimate actions she had considered clichés before she met Dowson, and submitted to them gladly. He had told her he loved her and she had told him, not while they were in bed, but when they were dressed, standing by the shutters in that first moment of fear between lovers when the actions are still. She had cried, of course, holding him close, then he had left her alone for a while before they met Leith together. She had walked around the room slowly, touching the chair, the wall, the bed itself, recording the pattern, every shadow, the very texture of the experience, in case it never happened again. She felt, she said, unworthy of anything more.

'What happened to Melissa?' Dowson asked.

'Abandoned the zombie,' Leith replied. 'Abandoned her. Statutory rape I can fight. Idiocy I can put up with. But mental and physical rigor mortis, old sport—what does a man do with that? Last time I saw her she was hitch-hiking to Turkey with Rasputin. Believe me, I felt about as necessary as Peter Pan's razor.'

Emily laughed and squeezed Dowson's arm.

'I tell you, Emily,' Leith continued, 'Jack Barrymore and I and a few others used to smoke that stuff before she was even born, but not twenty-four hours a day. All I got out of it were two Polaroids of her sitting on a rock like Buddha's daughter, and they're probably as out of focus as I was. God help me,' he said turning to Dowson, 'I felt like Mickey Methuselah out there and I missed you, Christopher, I really did.'

Dowson blushed and asked: 'Why didn't you come back then? The same day.'

'Too drunk. I'd have sunk the boat and gone down with it. Like Keats.'

'Shelley. Keats died in Rome.'

'So have I. A hundred times. The poor bastard.'

Leith talked for about an hour and both Dowson and Emily knew that they couldn't abandon him now, nor, in truth, did they want to. Neither of them had dared discuss the eventual departures from the island and so accepted the present moment with gratitude. Once, when Leith left them inevitably to find the toilet, Dowson anticipated Emily's question by saying:

'We must stay with him now, even for a couple of hours. He will not demand it but we can't leave him alone.'

'But has he no friends—I mean anywhere?'

'I don't know. The friends he talks about are dead. He has a wife I believe, but he never mentions her. You and I are his friends.'

'I want to be alone with you,' Emily said. 'I am as selfish as that.'

'Two hours,' Dowson replied. 'Lunch, a walk, then he will sleep. He has brought me here and he is entitled to that.'

But they wouldn't entitle him to that and they both knew it. Leith insisted that they should be alone and walked away, saying that he ought to supervise the boat. They both emphasized that they wanted to remain in his company but Leith merely grinned, hugged them, and said: 'Later. Dinner for three and you may have Leith grace your table again,' and lurched away, without looking back.

When Emily and Dowson returned to the hotel room, they stood by the bed (now remade, one pillow placed emphatically on its partner) and undressed silently, self-consciously, placing their clothes neatly on a chair, and Dowson got into bed first and looked at her. She didn't move, not even closing the shutters, but stood, naked, by the window, aware of his gaze, aware of her breasts (too small, a source of humiliation as a young girl), pleased at the absence of stretch-marks but conscious of her thighs, and when there was a knock on the door she made no reaction. It was almost inevitable.

Dowson pulled on his trousers and opened the door a few inches, masking her from the outside. The bar-waiter stood in the corridor, a look of irritated helplessness on his face:

'Signor Dowson, your friend—from the bar ... he asks for you.'

'Is he ill?'

'Yes. He is in the street and apologizes but ... '

Behind Dowson, Emily reached for her clothes as he closed the door.

'Don't come with me,' Dowson said. 'It would embarrass him.'

'Do you want me to wait here?'

'Perhaps you ought to go to your house. I will have to look after him for a while. I will see you later.'

'But *will* you?'

Dowson looked at her, the slight fear in her eyes, then smiled and walked towards her and kissed her gently on her neck. Emily immediately put her arms around him and held him tightly.

'Don't go,' she said. 'Leith would understand. You could say the waiter couldn't find us.'

Dowson looked over her shoulder, at their reflection in the mirror, her hair, her back, dalmatian shades of sun and shadow, the pallid mirage of her nakedness against him, the open window and the trees beyond and the harbour beyond that, not visible from here but if he was on the balcony he would see the boats, the yachts and then the two-master. A poem was written on hotel notepaper by his bed, a wedding ring was touching his waist, a woman with blonde hair, a mother of four children, was kissing his shoulder, murmuring his name. Outside, a man, almost sixty years old, was lying in a gutter.

'Now, we are *all* human, old sport,' Dowson said, unsmiling, closing the shutters. Returning to bed.

*   *   *

It is difficult for me to piece together the immediate events that followed, since Emily wrote no further letters home, nor indeed to anyone, and had already abandoned her diary. She admitted that she experienced a deep sense of guilt, though I knew it was not solely for the affair itself. It had perhaps something to do with Leith (in fact, I am certain of it) but the true moment of remorse for ignoring Leith that afternoon came to Emily many months later, as these things do, in retrospect, when the moment has gone.

There are episodes in my own life (I will refrain from counting) that still haunt me, when I have denied the smallest acts of kindness to others, often to those I love, which I try to forget, finding excuses in stubborn platitudes. Sometimes I succeed in convincing myself that such frailties are common to us all, that the hair-shirt is an absurd and somewhat outmoded act of atonement, but incidents recur, quite suddenly (a letter found at the back of a drawer, a name overheard from another part of the room, an orchestrated echo of a past summer, such sidelong glances as these), and I am vulnerable once more. I dwell on this too much, I realize, so I will cease. I am not in the confessional box, nor is Emily. It is mere speculation, for I have no facts, and consequently this emphasis on an incident which, after all, is understandable, is perhaps unfair. You have already suspected that I am not totally impartial, so I will admit it.

What is *not* surmise, however, is that Emily and Dowson visited Leith on his yacht that evening and found him asleep in his cabin. He had been carried there by two of the islanders, at his request, and had sent them away. When he awoke, there was no mention of the afternoon. He apparently just said he was pleased to see them both and that if they would allow him half an hour to shower and change, he would be fit and ready for dinner, as long as it wasn't fish. On no account would he eat fish on dry land, especially, he emphasized, leaving the cabin towards the shower, smoked bloody kippers.

Darling Emmie, Yesterday we took the children to Heddingbourne for Easter as you have probably guessed from the postmark. Everyone—including Robert!—sends their love and especially the

*children. They are all well, though Victoria's bronchitis has
returned again. She went swimming when it was much too cold, and
that I am sure must have brought it on. But don't worry about it for
she is in good hands. We've just put her to bed and pampered her
with comics and Enid Blyton and so I am sure she'll be up in a day
or two.*

*I do hope you are happy, darling—and brown!—and we think
of you constantly. I know how wretched everything is, but I know all
will be well. Received your first letter and await the others, but the
postal service is simply awful so your letters will all probably arrive
at once and we'll spend hours reading them. Won't write more
as you can see I have enclosed letters from everyone and they insisted,
especially James, that I leave all the gossip to them.*

*But I pray for you and love you and though we want to see you
desperately, we know that you must stay there as long as you wish to
think everything over. Am sorry all the others have gone away but
the islanders are very kind and I'm sure you are already making
friends. But Emmie, don't worry too much about Edward. Daddy
and I always hate each other every seven years and we're still
together! I have every hope.*

Love and hugs, MAMA

*Don't forget you can always phone and reverse the charges. We'll
be here till Saturday so please, please, do.*

But she never phoned and when Emily tried to write, she
found she could say nothing. Everything she *could* say was
either too important or too trivial to put in a letter. She sent
cards to the children, however, covering them with kiss-
crosses, sitting in her living-room, late that night, waiting
for Dowson to come and collect her.

They had arranged to sail to Dubrovnik, since both had
been told that the only time to see it was at dawn, when the
streets were empty. 'It's supposed to be like walking into the
Middle Ages,' Leith had said, 'like a dream, unreal and

61

empty except for ourselves,' and Emily had insisted that they go that night. Together. She wanted only to return to her house, which she hadn't visited for over twenty-four hours, to change her clothes and see, perhaps, if there were any letters from home.

When Dowson arrived, he realized immediately that she had been crying and then saw the letters and the children's drawings on the table.

'You don't have to go,' he said, sitting next to her. 'If you prefer to stay here alone ... '

'No ... ' Emily replied, embarrassed to be seen like this and looked away, staring out across the room. Dowson touched her arm and it was cold and there was no reaction and then he saw that she was trembling, almost like a child in fear. He felt helpless, unable to say anything and they sat, not looking at each other, the silence disturbed only by a mosquito and then by some tourists who were laughing and running in the street below and then they were gone.

Dowson stared at the drawings in front of him, signed by unfamiliar names, and at the letters, the alien intimacies, pages containing gestures, references, asides, that were as remote to him as a planet. A snapshot of two small boys and two small girls (one of them holding an Easter egg) whom he would have overlooked in a small room, and yet they had been given birth by this woman next to him, had been named and clothed and raised, had been worried over and loved by her, but they meant nothing to him. Nothing at all. They belonged to her alone, and a husband she avoided mentioning, and not to him. And they never really could. He was in love with, and had made love to, their mother and that was all. He was an intruder, a stranger to all that lay spread out before him and he wanted to leave.

Emily had said she needed him and he believed it. She asked him to give her strength that very afternoon as they lay in bed, and she had cried and told him of her life. Or at least some of it. Names had been mentioned, but they had been faceless, transparent images, like lists carved on a village war-memorial — emotive but meaningless to the traveller passing by. A husband she no longer loved, parents, friends, cousins, dogs, aunts, children. A shattered tapestry of scenes, incidents, figures, landscapes: frescoes of a life on a wall, unrelated, overlapping, some fading, some preserved and retouched with care, some simply kept in darkness. He himself had not talked of divorce or marriage, nor, in truth, even considered it, but that was the way it was. Dowson didn't resent this involvement, for he knew he was in love with her, but it had only been two days, three at the most, and Celia whom he had loved also was still with him, though she was no longer alive. He had never mentioned her to anyone, even to Emily, and there was perhaps fear in that also. The commitment. *Do you remember England?* Too well.

A silence. Dowson got up to leave slowly, and yet the action seemed to disturb the whole room. He sensed her turn and then cling to him, hiding her face (a letter is brushed aside. Falls to the floor) and then he heard her murmur:

'Victoria has got bronchitis again. I told her not to go swimming, but you know how stubborn she is.'

There is nothing more to say.

*   *   *

When Dowson returned to the yacht alone, the light was already separating sea from sky with a pale midriff of bronze, and he could hear the pulsating rattle of engines from the fishing boats. Leith was waiting on deck, still awake, though he may well have slept during the night.

'Emily not coming with us?' he asked.

Dowson didn't reply and sat down on one of the chairs

and lit a cigarette. Behind him, Leith stared at the harbour then at Dowson, then shrugged sympathetically.

'Well ... ' he said quietly. 'It's too late for Dubrovnik anyway. Another time.'

'Yes,' replied Dowson.

'Everything ... all right?'

'Of course. She just needed me to stay with her for a while. She was a little depressed. Her daughter's not well.'

'Nothing serious, old sport?'

'No,' said Dowson quickly. 'It'll go in a couple of days. Slight bronchitis ... '

'Oh yes. I used to have that—and look at me now,' and Leith coughed dramatically and grinned. Then he sat down on an adjacent chair and put his feet up on the rail and they both gazed at the horizon until the crest of the sun was visible. Silhouettes of boats passed before them, casual greetings, and voices could be heard, even at this hour, from the market-place and the steps below. Finally Leith said:

'Well now, what are our plans today? It looks as though it's going to be fine. Maybe the three of us could go swimming. Not nude, of course. Respectable.'

'I can't swim. But I can paddle, I suppose.'

Leith smiled:

'All right. For today, you can be captain. *You* decide.'

Dowson glanced at Leith then nodded and said:

'Fine. Emily should be here by noon.'

When Emily awoke, after taking a sleeping tablet, it was already eleven o'clock in the morning and the sun was dazzling her eyes. Despite everything, she felt contented now and relaxed and decided to put on her brightest dress (the yellow) and wear her hair loose, as Dowson preferred. Today, she resolved, she would attempt to acquire a suntan, that tiresome requisite of the English abroad, and so accordingly took a bikini from a suitcase. Emily had optimistically bought two before she left from a local boutique — a modest brown for when she was white, and a minuscule white affair for when she was brown. She, Dowson and Leith could sunbathe on the deck of the boat and perhaps sail round the island as had been suggested and find a restaurant in Lumbarda or Vela Luka. It would be *her* treat, she had told Dowson before he left the night before, a gift to them both.

She arrived at the harbour at noon, as was arranged, to discover that Dowson had already changed the plans. They had not been definite, merely a suggestion, but nevertheless she was disappointed since the boat was no longer there. There had been no note at her house nor was there any message at his hotel or at the *Planjak*. The boat simply was not there. She did not inquire at the harbour, nor did she need to, for she knew, even in the moment of waking, that Dowson had left the island forever, and was sailing south back to Italy. That, in fact, he had gone.

Two hours later, Emily took the steamer to Dubrovnik and then a plane back to England. As she told her mother, she couldn't bear not seeing the children before the school holidays were over. Surrounded by her children and her family, a picnic on the downs, kite-flying. Everyone knew she always looked forward to that.

Part Two

LEITH

Five

The events that I am about to describe, and many which have already been written, are false. That, may I hasten to add, is not because I have deliberately invented incidents that did not happen, but simply because I have not recorded other incidents that have.

By 'incidents', I mean each waking moment, each minute of a person's day – the trivialities, the walking, the eating, the whole timetable of each particular hour, from sunrise to sunset and then beyond. To do so, and I am sure it would not be impossible, would naturally be lengthy, pedantic and ultimately very dull. A death, a sudden tragedy, a moment of ecstasy, the rare peaks and depressions of life would appear, like an infinite chorus-line, amid the repetitions of washing, yawning, dressing, standing still, and all the commonplace activities that complete a person's day, yours and mine. They would wait their turn as each mundane second was set down, identified, tagged and passed by (the image of a conveyor belt comes to mind easily enough though that, on reflection, is not quite an accurate allusion) and then they themselves would appear, be identified, tagged in equal manner and then remorselessly be passed by once more. It would be accurate undoubtedly and perhaps interesting as an experimental curio, but in the end soporific (at least to me) and unreadable. There would be no balance. The flick of an eyelash would be equal in tempo and emphasis to the death of a son.

Every artist knows this elementary fact. Indeed everyone who is not an artist and yet communicates to another, whether it be gossip or reportage, knows it also. So we select. We choose the highlights, the crossing-stones from point to point, the basic relevancies in what we are presenting and attempt to achieve that as honestly and as dramatically as possible. Often, like the cartoonist or the poet, we attain truth more by elimination than by what is shown. I could elaborate more, but the point has been made.

As a writer I have so far set down what happened between two people (Emily, Dowson), the protagonists of this story, over a period of four months between November 1967 and March 1968. Now and again I have made assumptions on inner thoughts (much of which I learnt first hand) and sometimes I have attempted interpretations and judgments. I have avoided what is superfluous, except to add atmosphere, and concentrated solely on what is important in the understanding of a relationship, and within that, the people themselves. There, to return to my first statement, is the falsehood, or to be accurate, there is not the total truth.

For those mundane seconds that I have ignored may give deeper insight into what is about to happen, and why it happens, than what I have chosen to write. I cannot say if that is so, but they might. A gesture, a phrase that is considered insignificant by me, may well reveal all to someone else. If that is so, then it is to be regretted. My only defence is that I have been entrusted with all the diaries, letters, memories, taped conversations, personal observations I can find – anecdotes alone from two people (yet to appear) run to volumes – and have selected not only what I believe is accurate and just (though the law of libel has censored some. Not much, but some), but also, since this is intended to be a commercial assignment, how it ought to be written.

Having said the above (a justification to myself alone perhaps), let me say that I am now skipping unashamedly all of the months of April and of May, as well as at least two weeks of June. Also, we are no longer in Korčula nor in England, but in Rome. More particularly in a villa on the

Appia Antica. A haze, blurred colours, then we observe:

A young boy, nineteen years old, is lying face down on a white plastic inflatable sofa, floating, drifting gently across a swimming-pool the size of a carriage park. Now and then when the air is still, the heat hovers, he lowers a hand into the water and moves himself and the sofa slowly back across the width of the pool, or to the tiled edge itself where a glass of Mateus waits for him. The ice-cubes in the glass are pink, purple and malachite, small plastic boxes the size of dice, filled with ice that is rapidly melting (the heat hovers), turning the wine warm under a late morning sun. The boy is naked except for a strip of faded denim covering his thighs, his skin is the colour of Regency leather, his hair long and blond, the edges wet, a study in pastels, of impressionist colours, brown, white and mazzarine. Around him drift another sofa and two armchairs, white also, but empty, nudging each other as they are caught by a breeze, a floating living-room designed by Magritte (a pair of sunglasses lies at the bottom of the pool, abandoned) and the boy perhaps by Hockney. A surrealist canvas in which he belongs, as he knows. He has been there all morning, not moving, except to turn over, glance around the garden, raise an arm, a *Ciao*, to a man standing on the terrace, then close his eyes.

Lawns, occupied by sprinklers that relentlessly turn back and forth, forward and back, soothing arcs of sound, patterns of water beneath magnolia trees bearing white flowers large enough to fill an urn. A waiter picks up a glass, others lay a table in the shade against a backdrop of clematis, vines and wistaria. A patio of tiles copied from Pompeii, occupied at present by lizards, tubs of terracotta, a bust of an emperor (Tiberius) in an alcove, sightless. The heat hovers above distant chatter from the terrace, a sudden laugh, a man with grey hair and blue jeans appearing suddenly from the shadows of the villa itself, stopping, gazing at the pool, hesitating, then returning into the house. After a moment, a piano is heard, played perhaps by him, a limpid pavane by Ravel, played well, with confidence and affection.

Across the lawn, reached by a spine of paving stones meandering between flowers, is a table-tennis table, its surface blistered, the net torn, neglected, and beyond that some cushions (mauve, turquoise) and chairs that have been placed out of range of the sprinklers for guests to lie on and snooze and drink or merely daydream. In a hammock, within earshot and conspicuous, a man in a prawn-pink shirt and white cotton trousers, sunglasses pushed on to the top of his head, awaits to refuse an audience; he is an Italian who was called a genius twenty years ago and sees no reason to dispute the slander. He does not live in this house, nor in the Vatican, but in Venice, where he will return the next day, with the boy in the pool (they have not yet met but they both know) if the air becomes cool. But at the moment, the heat clings, suffocates, breeds fantasies.

Before and beneath the hammock, a woman on a cushion, pretty, red-haired, a slight sun-burn (inevitable with such colouring) who is anxiously bored. She has chosen a bikini a size too small, so that her nipples can be glimpsed by any-one standing over her, and is smoking some inferior hash that has been passed to her by a neighbour. She is American, recognizable to even the most casual film-goer, has never reached the status of star, is too old to be a starlet, and has been at the villa for the past six days, so it has been said. It is also said that the night before she was stripped and made love to by two men on that lawn that is at present out of sight behind the building, and had then scampered bare-bottomed on to the Appia Antica itself. But such gossip is usually unreliable, and besides, the actress has a husband in Singapore.

We have overlooked a dog, two dogs in fact, a composer,

a poet, four other actors, two army cadets (one out of uniform) from the neighbouring barracks, a young English writer who is waiting to discuss a film about Savonarola (of all people), a quartet of limpets from the Piazza del Popolo who gesture in hyperboles, a lime tree, an uninvited statue, two Alfa-Romeos and a photograph of the Rome football team. We have also ignored the group posing on the terrace above, which includes the host himself (middle-aged, vain, his gaze constantly jump-cutting between crotch and mouth); a designer of masks, the owner's secretary (a plain girl, grateful for anything); a film-producer of epics whose latest, the *Iliad*, convinced the viewer that the only thing he shared in common with Homer was his blindness; an actress of remarkable beauty who ought not to be there; a third-rate director (he was responsible for the aerial sequences in *Orpheus in the Underworld*) and an actor from England in love with his mirror. Another dog, and finally Dowson himself, sitting apart from the others, not ignoring them, but merely watching across the gravel driveway towards the entrance.

He becomes aware of the host, Baculi, as he approaches him, an unlit cigarette in his mouth, and stands next to him, one hand caressing a flower on the balustrade.

'Are you bored, Christopher?'

'No.'

'But you do not speak to us, Christopher?'

'I am waiting for a friend of mine.'

'But we are *all* your friends here.'

'I am waiting for a friend of mine called Leith.'

'And who is this Leith?'

'An actor.'

'Another one, Christopher?'

'Yes. Another one.'

*   *   *

Leith was drunk. It was still morning and yet he was drunk. Faced with the prospect of meeting people whose films he had never seen, whose names he couldn't pronounce and who seemed to live in a world floating above him, like Laputians, he had drunk a full bottle of vodka and was beginning to regret it.

Dowson had prepared him for the encounter, had told him that their intellectual charades were farcical, a coterie of smug Dorian Grays whose true pictures were not in the attic but on celluloid and who professed to reveal the secret of the universe in the antics of a harlequin or a colouring-book monologue of Marx, and Leith had tried to accept that. It was reassuring but he was aware that he wasn't even educated enough to recognize those who were not, and so treated anyone who exhibited even a thumb-nail sketch of intelligence outside his range with a mixture of awe and inferiority. That was why, he knew, he avoided crowds, gatherings and cocktail parties and preferred the solitude of a boat at sea, especially now when he could no longer dominate a room by his appearance alone.

Twenty years ago, a studio would tell him what to do. Would give him a script and tell him to report on Monday. He had objected to most of the parts he had played, had begged to be allowed to appear in something other than jock-strap and tights (unless it was *Hamlet*), but at least then it had been all so simple. He admired his contemporaries who had fought the studio system and succeeded, but he himself wasn't like that, partly perhaps because he never really wanted to be an actor in the first place. He hadn't been discovered in a drugstore like Lana Turner, but in the bar next door, and that really was that. Now, after four wives, five children and thirty-eight films, he was back in the bar again, a curiosity, expecting any day to find his name listed in a magazine, in one of those innumerable articles on the preservation of rare species: *O for Okapi, P for Platypus,*

S for Swashbuckler. It was maudlin sentiment, Leith knew, and he attributed it to the alcohol, Roman driving and the never-ending frieze of cypress trees.

He was also frightened. There was no doubt about that. He had once been sent a script of *The Great Gatsby* (it was later given to Alan Ladd) and remembered a scene where Gatsby had been frightened at the thought of meeting an ex-mistress he still loved and had drunk himself into a stupor. He identified with that action then and he identified with it now. At times like this, he used to say, he needed a woman or a drink, and preferably both. He'd had the drink and he'd find the woman before the day was out, but he needed more than that now. He needed a job, a job he could respect, and these people in the villa ahead could give it to him. He was an actor, as his passport could prove, and though many of his films had been ridiculed, there were some moments, rare perhaps, but some, of which he wasn't ashamed. He had made, in his own way, a contribution to the cinema, had entertained millions in the past and no one could take that away. He could still walk (sometimes) and talk, appear on cue and remember his lines, and if his name no longer appeared above the title, only his pride suffered and not his bank-account, nor, in truth, his performance. But it was, when all things were considered, a bloody absurd way to make a living.

They were now approaching the villa and Leith could see the cars and one or two people on a lawn. He looked around anxiously for Dowson but couldn't find him, then got out of the car, burning his hand momentarily on the steel roof, paid the driver and stood nervously in the driveway, aware of the glances.

He became conscious of his suit, of his tie, his shoes (suede), the pocket handkerchief, the cufflinks, the mono-grammed *AL*. He began to sway, steadied himself and put a

cigarette in his mouth, his hand shaking, found he had forgotten his lighter and became terrified of moving. The path
to the garden seemed endless, ever-unfolding, and he knew
he could never make it. Behind him the taxi had turned and
had gone and he was abandoned. Faces peered at him, everyone seemed so underdressed, acres of bronzed flesh, boys
grinning, the heat shimmering around him, a chauffeur leaning against a car twenty yards away watching him, as if he
were a specimen on a slide, laughter, nicknames, sidelong
glances, fingers raised to mouths and Leith found himself
sweating, his skin cold, and then inevitably, he vomited,
turned away and vomited behind some potted plants. He
wanted to die, when suddenly there was a stillness, a breath-
less quiet except for the sound of his lungs returning to their
natural tempo. He stood up slowly and wiped his mouth on
the handkerchief and cautiously looked around. Nothing
had changed. The chauffeur was talking to a girl, a neighbour's child was smiling and waving to him from a swing
on the other side of the hedge; the villa lawn was empty
except for two people reading magazines and there was a
pleasant beauty about the shadows and the flowers, a lizard
darting suddenly into the undergrowth, and the carvings
above the door of the house.

'Hallo, Leith,' Dowson said, smiling and taking his arm.
'Everyone is round the back having lunch. You're just in
time,' and then smiled again and added: 'You look fine.
You really do.'

There were twelve people at the table on the patio (pasta
and green salad, steak tartare if preferred) who looked up
and across the lawns as Dowson approached with Leith.
One or two heads were put together, a hand thrown up in
surprise, a ripple of questions along the table, then the two
men stood before them. Leith looked at the faces who gazed
at him silently, one or two touching the corners of their

mouth or their chin with a napkin, another curling a side-
board of his hair between two fingers, then Dowson said:

'I'd like to introduce you to Arden Leith.'

Leith nodded and offered a hand, but he received merely
brief horizontal smiles, silent observations (someone asked
for the wine to be passed), then the guests returned to their
conversations, speaking in Italian, except the host himself,
who stood up and snapped a finger to a waiter for another
chair to be brought.

'When Christopher told me your name,' he said to Leith,
studying him, 'I never connected it with ... well, with you.'

Leith smiled shyly and Dowson said:

'I just referred to you as Leith. I knew everyone would
recognize you as soon as they saw you.' Then to Baculi:
'Leith hates to be called by his first name, except by women.'

'Ah yes,' replied Baculi, gesturing Leith to a chair placed
between him and a young actress everyone ignored. 'You
know a lot about women, I believe.'

'Very little, Mr ... '

'You must call me Donali.'

'Very little. In fact I know less about them every day.'

'But you have had many wives.'

'Exactly.'

Dowson smiled at Leith and nodded encouragement and
sat opposite him, seemingly unaware of Baculi's hand resting
on his arm.

After a silence, then a further brief exchange, Leith was
ignored and cautiously helped himself to the wine. Once or
twice a question was directed at him in broken English or
American, questions he had heard many times before but
he found himself flattered by the attention: 'I saw you in
William Tell. Did you do all the action yourself? Which
film did you prefer? Are you really English or American?
(*English*.) Were you not in *Beau Geste*? (*No, that was Gary
Cooper*.) Then *Captain Blood*? (*No, that was Errol Flynn*.)

77

Did you ever meet Humphrey Bogart? (*Frequently.*) Did you like him? (*We were both too drunk to care.*) Did you do all the action yourself? (Leith has already answered that, Franco.) Did you ever meet Marilyn Monroe, James Dean, Greta Garbo? Which actress did you enjoy working with most? (*Olivia de Havilland and Lassie.*)

And then, when the wine was finished, then more wine and then the cognac and the sambuco, the questions became more personal as scandal was sought amid giggles and whispers. Did you really rape those two girls? (*It was called statutory rape which is a different thing. Even if a girl consents and rapes you, if she's under eighteen the law considers it rape. Besides, I was acquitted. I have never needed to rape anyone in my life.*) Such a pity. Que dommagio. What is your greatest fear? (*Castration.*) Your greatest fuck? (*The next one.*) Is it true what they say? What *do* they say? You know, what they say? No, tell me what they say. About the size of your cock? (*That is one thing I assure you, you will never find out.*)

'But *she* might,' said Baculi, pointing to the young actress, speaking for the first time.

'Not now, old sport,' smiled Leith. 'Not now.'

'Old sport? What is this—old sport?' Baculi cried suddenly, startlingly, in a falsetto of dramatic outrage. 'Why does he call me "old sport"? I am not old, nor am I this "sport".'

A puzzled silence after the realization that this was no longer a joke. For ten minutes Baculi had been ignored. There was a restrained snigger. A chair falling backwards noisily to the tiles as a man moves away, suppressing a laugh. A concentration of attention on a glass, a tree, a dog moving across the lawn.

'It's a phrase,' Dowson said calmly, lighting Baculi's cigarette. 'That's all. Leith calls everyone he likes "old sport". As you might say *caro amico* or whatever. It's an English phrase.'

78

'I have never heard of it before. "Old sport". What is that?

'I'm sorry—' Leith began.

'Don't apologize,' said Dowson emphatically. 'You need not apologize.'

Baculi looked at Leith for a long time, his face flushed, then carefully placed his napkin on the table, stood up and looked at the others left at the table as if Dowson and Leith no longer existed.

'Il pranzo è finito!' he said, slapping his hands together hard, then strode across the lawn, followed by the guests, his arms around two of them as they tried to console him, then resisting them and throwing his hands up in the air. Dowson and Leith were left alone except for the young actress (Antonella) who stared ahead of her, lower lip under upper teeth, glancing at Dowson constantly.

'They're very temperamental,' said Dowson finally, refilling Leith's glass and selecting an orange. 'Italians like that. Look at him. He thinks he's at La Scala. *Bruta figura*.'

The girl smiled and repeated the phrase in agreement:

'*Bruta figura* … '

'Loss of face,' Dowson continued. 'He's a vain man. That is all.'

Leith was stunned.

'Does that mean … I've thrown away the job?' he asked apologetically.

Dowson hesitated then gazed slowly around the garden. The man in the hammock was still there, having not been at the table, since he refused to share second billing with the host. The boy was still in the pool also, but sitting up now, a willing cynosure for the guests who stood on the edge of the water, like gallery visitors before a roped-off masterpiece.

'Not yet,' murmured Dowson. 'Not quite just yet.'

He then got up, chewing at a slice of orange, and placed the chair under the table.

'You won't be long, will you?' Leith asked anxiously.

'No, old sport,' Dowson grinned. 'I'll be back. If you want to be alone, there are plenty of rooms in the villa.'

He then began to walk away, across the garden towards the far lawn beyond. Halfway there, he heard someone running after him and turned to see the girl, Antonella.

'Can I come with you?'

'You don't know where I'm going.'

'I just want to be with you. I feel like a freak here. You know what I mean.'

Dowson looked at her, then past her to where Leith was sitting, isolated, very alone, pouring himself another cognac.

'What is your name?'

'Antonella.'

'Look after him, Antonella,' Dowson said, gesturing towards Leith. 'He can't get you into films, nor make you famous, nor introduce you to Paul Newman. But he's a friend of mine from England. Talk to him.'

'Are you sure that he'd want to? I mean — just talk?'

'I don't know. Why don't you ask him?'

Antonella nodded, looked back at the table. She was wearing jeans and a white tee-shirt and a man's leather belt. Hazel eyes, wide mouth, English despite her name, a nose that was the envy of plastic surgeons but was in fact given to her by her mother. Good breasts, bra-less, a model's hips and legs, bare feet, a slight hammer toe.

'All right,' she said, then added quickly to Dowson: 'You're not queer as well are you? I mean like the others.'

Dowson laughed, startling her, and said:

'Everyone asks me that,' then walked away.

Six

In England, or more particularly, in Cumberland, the weather in May had been unpredictable. For the first week the sky had been cloudy, hovering low over the lake, a gouache of mists on the water obscuring the hills beyond, and then finally it had rained and Emily was confined to the house and the fire was lit in the main hall. She was not alone (this being her parents' house), having the company of her mother and her elder brother, but she saw them rarely during the daytime. Antony would leave early to go riding or visit friends in neighbouring villages, and her mother seemed to be involved in interminable committee meetings, opening bazaars, representing her husband at functions he carefully avoided.

At first, they attempted to take her with them, planning excursions to Grasmere or to dine with the Brookfields, but Emily seemed reluctant and so they left her alone, unwillingly but with sympathy. They simply assumed that she wanted to think, to work matters out for herself, and in the evenings they all went to bed early, turning out the lights and leaving the Scrabble board and the unfinished jigsaw on the drawing-room table.

Dowson was never discussed, of course, for indeed they knew nothing about him or even of his existence. Emily had decided to tell them if a letter arrived, but it never did. Each morning since leaving Korčula, she had stage-managed an indifference at the breakfast table when the day's mail was brought in by Deverell and placed beside her plate; she would glance quickly at the white envelopes, the defiant

English postage stamps, the invitations, and then leave them unopened.

Once, unexpectedly, at the end of April, after the three eldest children had been sent back to school, her brother passed her an air-mail letter that had been given to him by mistake. 'This one's for you. All the way from Yugoslavia,' and then added: 'Aren't you going to open it? Might be from Marshal Tito,' and Emily had taken it quickly, nervously, and read it alone in her room. It was from her cousin, regretting that he had missed her, hoping that she had had a good time with the Jugos and that he would no doubt see her at Fiona's ghastly wedding. After that, she expected nothing and tried to adjust herself to the idea that she would never see Dowson again. He knew her address and he hadn't written. She felt no bitterness, no regret at what had happened; she was simply alone, and after a while she realized that she couldn't even remember his face, the shape of his nose, the tone of his voice. There were merely oblique memories, gestures, the emptiness that pervaded her whole body, and the love itself. The embroidered bag was placed in a drawer, next to her diary, and two dresses (a yellow and a blue decorated with fuchsias) remained in the darkness of the wardrobe hidden by winter furs.

At one time she began to write down her thoughts, as a form of therapy, but abandoned it after a page and then it was burnt. She would spend hours with her youngest child, Annabelle, who was too young to be at boarding-school, reading Beatrix Potter, taking walks in the garden and the fields beyond, revisiting a bridge, a house, a grove of pine-trees that had been her own childhood. She would stand on a hill and see the house below, her mother in the garden inspecting the yew hedges, the lake, and decided that she never wanted to leave Cumberland; she had spent the first seventeen years of her life here, and when she had left it, it had been to marry Hallam and by marrying him and leaving him, she had met Dowson. There had at least been a security, a protection in the adolescent vacuum. False, and unnatural perhaps, but it could be recaptured.

In May therefore, she moved back to the bedroom she occupied as a child (an oval room in Regency stripes with prints by Rackham on one wall) and began to read the books she had read at school, inscribed with her maiden name, *Emily Charlotte Bowness*, on the inside cover. She suggested games, treasure-hunts that she had played with her brothers when they were young, slept with a doll by her pillow, and once put on a party dress, designed for her presentation debut, and wore it to dinner. For a while, in this reincarnation of her virginity, she appeared to be happy and went shopping with her mother in Buttermere and visited the cottagers on the estate for tea and cakes, who told her she hadn't changed and offered her the best chair.

When it finally rained, the jigsaws were taken from the nursery and the familiar pieces (many lost) were reassembled (a view of Tintern Abbey was a particular favourite), then returned to their box. Her mother observed these early weeks, first with apprehension, then relief as she saw her daughter slowly emerging from her shell, though she was not unaware that by doing so, Emily was re-entering another shell, more familiar perhaps, but distressing. She said nothing, however, putting aside her fears, and encouraged the fantasies, the retreats to infancy, for she could offer no alternative. Emily seemed unwilling to confide in her, to talk about anything that had happened in the past decade except the children themselves. So they continued the charades in the evenings, revisited the attics and the basements, reminisced in undertones and played out the pitiful pretence of it all.

A favourite game, for example, was Quotations. Emily had always been well-read, surprising even the most intellectual adult with her knowledge of esoteric books and used to gleefully sit on the edge of her chair as extracts from novels, poems were read out to be guessed. Her expertise at sixteen was considered quite remarkable, and she had stunned everyone (a Member of Parliament, three cousins and dear Aunt Mab) by identifying a book on hearing the very last word alone. The word in fact was *jardin*; the book, *Candide*.

So one evening, they played Quotations, the three of them in the drawing-room (Deverell bringing in tea), sitting with anthologies and prepared paragraphs. The first sentence of *Anna Karenina* was a natural success for all; Jane Austen, as usual, produced a mere hesitation over the book itself (*Emma*) while *Parade's End* and something from Waugh were Emily's *coup de grâce*. The game moved to poetry, on the basis that it was more difficult. Poets could be identified perhaps, but the poem itself was a different matter. Her mother began:

> *Far are the shades of Arabia*
> *Where the princes ride at noon ...*

'Browning,' said Antony, guessing wildly. 'Robert, not Elizabeth.'

'Neither!' shouted Emily, sitting giggling on the floor, the family dog by her side. 'It's Walter de la Mare. And I'll tell you the poem. I know De la Mare well. Wait a minute. "All That's Past." '

'Wrong. Right poet. Wrong poem.'

'Hell! Then it must be "Arabia". Of course.'

It was. The game progressed, Deverell retired to bed, the curtains were drawn, lamps lit in corners. Rupert Brooke, Pound, de la Mare again, Betjeman (too easy. A point to Antony), Pushkin.

'All right, Emmie,' said Antony. 'My turn. You'll recognize it but who wrote it? It's very famous.'

'Tell me. Oh stop it, Grumble! Mama, Grumble's much too fat. Tell me.'

'All right. *And I was desolate and sick of an old passion.* There.'

Silence. A concentration of thought, a frown, a demand for it to be repeated: *And I was desolate and sick of an old passion.* A hazardous guess: 'Keats?'

'No,' said Antony, smiling. 'Point to me.'

'Who is it then?'

'Told you you wouldn't get it.'

'All right. But I'm still winning. Tell me who it is.'

'Dowson,' replied Antony, holding up the book as proof. 'Ernest Dowson. 1867 to 1900. So there.'

*   *   *

It could not be avoided. The echoes, the remembrances from innocent conversations. A drawing of a man in a white suit in a collection of the *Illustrated London News*, a boat ticket, a dinar found in a pocket, the sound of the gardener mowing the lawn in the early morning. *Curtains disturbed gently, a chair with her dress on its lap, a single shoe, a print (sepia) framed on the opposite wall, sheep wandering amid ruins.* His presence entered the house itself, and then her room and her bed, and if she could banish his image from her day, it would return in her dreams at night, or suddenly walking across a lawn, buying cigarettes from a corner shop, tasting a glass of wine, she would see him, not clearly, but within her eyeline. She would turn on the stairs then return to her room and stare out of the window at the empty driveway. The games were abandoned, the doll replaced in the cupboard, and by the middle of May, Emily left the oval room, choosing to sleep in another. At one point she almost told everything to her mother but stopped and changed the subject and put on her yellow dress when the weather cleared and there was sunshine. She would be seen walking alone along the side of the lake, between a row of elms, wearing a straw hat, the dog, Grumble, at her heels.

At the end of the month, she left Cumberland altogether.

'Martha's asked me to stay with her at Stadshunt,' she told her mother. 'There's just her and Rupert and I thought I'd go. For a few days at least, until the kiddies' half-term.'

Antony drove her to the station at Keswick and bought her a newspaper and some magazines (*Country Life, House & Garden*), and they sat on a bench on the platform with Annabelle, waiting for the train, joking shyly about trivial things.

'How long will you stay here?' Emily asked finally, clutching a bag in front of her, gazing across the lines at the fence, the grey stone, and the fields beyond.

'Three more days. Got to return to the camp by Monday.'

'Do you know where they are sending you?'

'Can't say. You know that. But if I return with a sun-tan, you'll know it won't be Alaska.'

'No ... I'll know that.'

Then they were silent and watched a porter on the opposite platform rolling a cigarette, very expertly with his fingers, then light it, hands cupped around the tip. Her brother then grinned heartily and asked Emily if Annabelle wanted any chocolate but the child was asleep and Emily shook her head. He looked at his watch again and nodded and was silent. A man and a woman appeared and stood and looked at a timetable near-by then along the railway track.

'It'll be all right ... ' Antony said finally, not looking at her. 'You mustn't get so depressed. I mean you know what I feel about Hallam, but things might change. Remember when I was in love with that creature from Yorkshire —'

'Jane Oakes?'

'Jane Oakes! Thought the world would end when she married Leyburn. Bloody Leyburn of all people. Used to

be my fag, used to thump his mucky knickers, and she goes
and marries the bugger.'

'Is she happy?'

'Suppose so. Well — when his father dies, she'll get a title
and that's really what she wanted. Lady Leyburn — can you
imagine it? I've got photographs of her that would knock
her right out of Burke's Peerage in one go.'

Emily laughed then said:

'Well, it's your own fault. You'll get a title as well.
Eventually.'

'That's what I told her, but she worked out that Leyburn
senior would die before Dad. Mercenary lot, aren't we?'

A silence again. The train was late and both of them
found that they had nothing more to say. They were embarrassed because they loved each other and Emily knew that
she could never tell Antony anything, not because he
wouldn't be sympathetic, but because he might not understand. However she described Dowson, in his eyes he could
only be seen unfavourably, a drifter who had made love to
his sister then disappeared, and she couldn't bear to hear
that. Instead, Emily looked at her daughter, sleeping in a
fold-up chair beside them, and carefully covered her feet
with a blanket that had fallen away.

'Looks just like you,' Antony said suddenly.

'Is that a compliment?'

'Oh God, yes. To both of you.' Then: 'You know if
there's anything I can do ... I know I'm not much use
sometimes, never here, but well, I am your brother and ... '

He then blushed and shrugged and searched for a cigarette.

'I know,' replied Emily. 'Don't worry.'

'Well — if I saw Hallam now, I'd kick his bloody teeth in
for what he's doing to you.'

'It isn't Edward,' Emily said quietly.

A pause, then her brother looked at her, holding the unlit
cigarette, looked at her for a long time, then took her hand:

'Oh, Emmie ... '

They didn't talk any more until the train finally arrived and Antony carried his niece to an empty carriage, then placed Emily's suitcase on the rack.

'Goodbye, Emily. Give my love to old Benenden.'

'I will.'

'I'll write to you from far-off places.'

'Please do.'

Then the train moved away and Emily stood and watched her brother on the platform, not moving, very still, till he was out of sight and they were moving east then south, through hills, towards Warwickshire.

She sat in the corner of the compartment and gazed at the passing hills and lakes, a glimpse of her house as always, then the woods and in time they would be in Westmorland and entering the Dales of Yorkshire. There is always a sense of pathos about English trains moving through English countryside that I myself have found is experienced by many, especially when one is travelling alone. There is no rational explanation for this — as there is no rational explanation why graveyards should be sensual or spiders should produce omens of death — except a purely emotional response. One may be, indeed, ecstatically happy, en route to see a lover or a treasured friend, but that pathos still seems to be there, despite everything. It is not surprising to me, therefore, that as Emily returned to the house where she first saw Dowson, she found that she was in tears. Whatever one may say about Dowson, favourable or not, the fact is that he never wrote to her once in the three months after abandoning her, and that he was aware, as Leith was aware, of the effect such apparent apathy could produce in a woman like Emily Hallam. Whatever the justification, whatever reasons you yourself might propose, no one forgave Dowson for that. No one at all. Except, of course, Emily herself.

Seven

Rome has never been a favourite city of mine. I realize that I am in the minority in my displeasure towards what is considered the holy of holies to everyone who is not obliged to put Mecca on the top of their tourist list, but there it is. I have no particular aversion that I can identify (the Pope himself has always waved to me whenever I have been passing by) so I assume it's simply a basic dislike for cities in general, and especially one that insists on being eternal.

The architecture is certainly intriguing, the history undeniable, and being a man of adequate means, I have explored the best and worst of the food and the night life, and have found the *vita* not quite so *dolce* as I had hoped. Admittedly, I have not visited every capital in the world (Bangkok has so far been neglected, while Canberra can well exist without me), but Rome, alas, is not to my taste. By saying this, I am echoing Leith's feelings alone, for I am not sure about Dowson. To be honest, in all my assessments of Christopher Dowson, I constantly find myself confronted by enigmas, paradoxes, sudden actions that, in contrast to his general character, are outrageously infantile. An example of what I mean will be described quite soon. Explanations can be found, even recorded, though regrettably, as far as Rome is concerned, most of his journal was burnt, and people I have talked to who knew him there were generally evasive, biased or blatantly hostile. Why Dowson should produce such anatagonism in people remains a mystery. And until further evidence is produced, I suppose it always will.

The afternoon at Baculi's for instance. Dowson had been

invited by at least four people, including the host himself, and had been propositioned by both sexes in the space of an hour. He had been as polite and considerate — especially to Leith — as always, had created no dramatic outbursts that can be recalled, and yet almost all who were present at the villa that day either refused to talk about him or attacked him with the vehemency usually employed by Church celebrities, Surrey mothers-in-law and wildebeeste. Despite that, facts were revealed.

Dowson had spent not only the whole day at the villa but also the night, after insisting that Leith (plus Antonella) return to their Roman hotel with the assurance that a part in a film had been promised. It was not discovered how the role had been secured, for Dowson refused to say, nor did Leith understand why his friend insisted on staying the night at Baculi's, knowing how much he loathed the people there. But that was the way it was; at least that was the way it ought to have been.

And yet, after two weeks, Leith still hadn't received either a script or a contract or even a note, and when he inquired through his agent, he received only oblique replies and self-conscious pleas for patience. He couldn't pursue the matter through Dowson himself, for he had suddenly gone away to visit Siena and Florence, alone, and had not yet returned. So Leith simply sat in the hotel with Antonella (a lover of great charm), visited the boat at Ostia and waited for the telephone to ring. Now and again he would dine on the Via Veneto, but abandoned that when he found that he was constantly in the company of other actors, mostly English and American, who had never achieved any real status in their career (nor deserved to) and who now sat on terraces, steps, the edges of fountains, framing a close-up of sun-tan, dark glasses and grey side-whiskers.

Once, out of natural vanity, he had accepted an invitation to a party given by an actor who had the dubious privilege of playing Tarzan of the Apes, but he and Antonella had left early. Leith had drunk as much as he could stand, had listened to all the pitiful opportunities each person in the room was expecting, and then left without saying goodbye. 'They think I'm just like them, sweetheart,' he had told Antonella in the lift. 'Pretending I've got a part when I haven't. They just don't want to believe me when I tell them it's almost signed and sealed.'

But after two more days, there was still no news and Leith began to drink more heavily than he had done for months, and twice collapsed in the street. He thought of revisiting the villa and finally did, but the gates were locked, the shutters closed and the garden empty.

He spent a day in bed with Antonella, nursed by her when he complained of a pain in his side, and she told him of her life in England; they discussed places they had both seen and enjoyed (Greenwich Museum, the hills of Dorset, Wilton) and he learnt how much of his native country had changed. He hadn't seen it at length for twenty years, except for brief visits to promote a film, attend a funeral, and that depressed him more than ever. The telephone remained silent and he made love to Antonella; not as often as he wished because he no longer had the strength, but with gentleness and affection. These qualities surprised her because she didn't expect them, since her previous lovers had always considered aggression and style to be the attributes a woman desired, and so she had been dissatisfied. With Leith, however, a man older than her father and at least two of her uncles, she experienced the sexual happiness that had always eluded her. 'Quality not quantity, sweetheart,' Leith had said grinning, posing before the shower one morning. 'Or, as you see, preferably both. But no photographs, please.'

But these were rare moments, for the love-making itself diminished in the detumescence of alcohol. The month of silence was a long time, and after a while, neither of them discussed the film that might happen, adopting the superstition that to mention it would automatically cancel it out. Instead, they went to the cinema, visited museums or simply stayed in the suite and watched television which neither of them could understand. Both wanted Dowson to return and talked about him, but they received no card or message and in a way, they resented that.

It appears that during those weeks, Leith first attempted to write his autobiography, preferring the realities of the past to the hypotheses of the future. A mere chapter was written, describing his childhood, and is in my possession now. I could quote from it, but it adds nothing of importance, except to confirm Leith's nostalgia (over-romantic at times, it must be said) for Suffolk and the village where he was born. There is one phrase which suggests the style: *Greenness green, like chartreuse, were the summers of my infancy. Greenness green and silent pines raped by a celluloid ego*, but it borders too much on a self-pity, understandable as that is.

I traced Antonella in 1970 (she is now married and still, as far as I know, living in Paris with a man called Catesby) and after her initial reluctance to talk, told me a few details about those few weeks in Rome. Most are what I have already written, but she did say that Leith talked incessantly about Dowson. He had told her how they had met in the Piazza Navona, about Korčula and the tour of the islands. Emily, however, was never mentioned (at least, not according to Antonella) though I know she must have been. 'He talked of Dowson as if he were his son and yet more than that,' Antonella had said. 'He loved him and he said this repeatedly, saying Christopher would do this, Christopher would know how to do that. He admired him and trusted him and when he wasn't there for that whole month, he said he was helpless as if he were blind. And he was.' Why then,

I asked, was Dowson disliked by so many in Rome who knew him?

'He was just too honest,' she said without hesitation. 'I think that's what it was. They couldn't cope with that—even me.'

Then she shrugged the thought aside, gave an embarrassed smile and seemed anxious to leave. Did *you* love Dowson? I asked. I remember she looked at me and at the note-pad on the table, then stared out at the traffic for a moment (we were lunching on the Boulevard St Michel. The café opposite the fountain), then replied as if admitting it for the first time:

'Yes. But he was in love with someone else.'

I questioned why she should say that. Did he say as much? Did he mention a name? But the interview was over. I paid the bill and she left and I have never seen Antonella again.

After ten more days, it was obvious to Leith that the chances of him being in the proposed film were remote. When he telephoned his agent's office, he found himself talking to the secretary, being told that everyone was still in conference or had just gone out, that they would of course phone back. They never did and he became angry, and once violent, though only to the extent of smashing a table-lamp. Such treatment from producers he could tolerate when he was young and unknown (though never forgive), but not now. He would go round to the offices in person, and once he was told by a young man who stared into space with an air of tolerant irritation (the air one usually reserves for a neighbour's child), that the director was in Venice and could not be contacted. Questions, threats, further questions produced only that Continental gesture of apathetic helplessness that makes murderers of us all (a raising of the shoulders, a pout, arms bent at the elbow, palms up as if frozen with an invisible skipping-rope).

Inevitably, Leith returned to the Via Veneto to the ageing Tarzans and Hercules and the obese producers in tinted glasses still peddling scripts that were originally written for Fatty Arbuckle; drifting from the tables at Doney's to the Café de Paris, shaking hands with Cassius and accepting a drink from Iago. He abandoned Antonella, abandoned everything in this binge, queued to lunch at the Taverna Flavia in order to sit facing the wall and then drank till it was dusk and the Fiats and the Lambrettas crammed the streets, visiting the bars in the Piazza del Popolo once and yet again.

He was recognized, of course, openly by tourists and he signed autographs to nieces in Omaha, and he knew that the leech on his left, the grub on his right were merely pitiful bookends to his ego and nothing more. But he remained, to repeat yet another anecdote: 'This bit-actor who always played the villain, always was killed in the third reel, decided to commit suicide in a fit of depression. Being an actor, he thought he'd do it in his next film. Die for real, actually die, old sport, right there on the screen with the cameras turning. He had worked out that he would exchange a prop knife for a real knife, that kind of thing. Waited anxiously for the next part, wrote his will, sold his house—and then, for God's sake, it turns out he's been offered a bloody comedy, where he not only is asked to survive but he gets the girl and has to live happily ever after. Dissolve. So, anyway, he did three weeks' shooting, all the close-ups, all the major scenes, then he goes and hangs himself in the bathroom with half the film still to go. Hangs himself. Dead. Well, old sport, everyone was upset of course—I'll tell you his name in a minute but can't think of it. Begins with *J*. Jimmy somebody. You'll know who I mean, Tony—everyone upset because, well, he was under contract to finish the film and it was too late to cover him. Should have done it on the first day, they said—would have saved the studio a fortune. They never forgave him for that—no. Just vodka, no ice—never did. Those were the days.' Drifted, he befriended sycophants, bitched at his successful contemporaries (*Look, I remember Hank Fonda before he was even* Little *Mr Lincoln*), and spent nights in remote apartments, watching blue movies supplied by a millionaire's son and his actress wife, making love to Contessas who insisted on calling him *Leef*, submitting willingly to the pathetic masturbation of it all. *Do you remember Hollywood? Old Sport?*

When Dowson returned finally from Florence, he found Antonella in Leith's bedroom with an Italian who claimed to work at Cinecittà.

'What's *he* doing here and where's Leith?' Dowson asked, slamming the door.

'I don't know—' Antonella replied nervously, moving across the bed, pulling a sheet over her breasts.

Dowson looked at the man in the bed, who was trembling, his eyes veering in panic towards a village saint, then looked back at Antonella.

'Has he started the film? Leith?'

'There *isn't* any film—'

'What do you mean there isn't any film? He was supposed to start last week!'

'There isn't any film, Christopher. Honestly. I think they gave the part to someone else.'

'Don't lie to me,' said Dowson and began to move across the room.

'I'm not lying to you. I'm not—'

'Did Leith try? Did he *try* to get the film?'

'Yes. *Yes!* He phoned every day. Twice a day. I was here. He went there, phoned—they just didn't want to know. Look, I know what these bastards are like. Believe me, Christopher—they almost killed him.'

Dowson didn't move for a long time, then slowly walked

to the bed and studied the Italian who was repeating 'Mi scusi, mi scusi', and holding up an arm against his face as if he were about to be hit. The room smelt of sweat, feet, cheap after-shave lotion and the decaying piscine odour of sex.

'Come si chiama?' asked Dowson, smiling, startling the Italian and pulling aside the bedclothes to expose the two bodies on the bed, legs angled ungainly and frozen like lava corpses in Pompeii.

'Pasquale,' the man blurted out.

'Parla inglese?'

'Si.'

Dowson nodded and casually studied the Italian's paunch, the legs, the hair that covered his skin from crotch to shoulders to feet.

'What do you do for a job, Pasquale?'

A stammer, then:

'I work ... I work Cinecittà.'

Next to him, Antonella tried to move, on the verge of tears, but Dowson seized her arm and pulled her out of bed, pulled her struggling and terrified and touched her breasts, her bottom, the triangle of moist hair, and then he slapped her across the face with such force that she ricocheted from one wall to the next. In the bed, the man didn't move, turning away, praying to his mother.

'I told you to look after Leith. This is his room, his hotel. That's all you had to do,' and Dowson moved towards the girl again and she began to tremble, hands seeking desperately the most vulnerable zone. 'Nothing else. Just look after Leith. So where is he?'

'I don't know ... I *did* look after him, but he disappeared and I don't know where he is. Oh God, don't hit me again.'

Dowson paused, looking into her eyes, then nodded and slowly moved a stray wisp of hair from her cheek and gestured to her to return to the bed. She flinched, then did so and he carefully covered her legs and thighs as if she were a baby. Then kissed the bruise that would soon appear.

'I'm sorry,' he said. 'I know.'

Then he walked to the door and opened it:

'You're not lying to me about Leith, are you? And the film?'

'No. I swear, Christopher. He said that the office laughed and told him to go away.'

A pause and Dowson was about to leave when Antonella said:

'Oh, Christopher – a woman called to see you two days ago.'

Dowson stopped, keeping his back to them.

'She was very disappointed that you weren't here,' Antonella continued.

'How old was she?'

'I don't know. Fifty perhaps. Very beautiful. She left you an envelope. In the drawer.'

Dowson hesitated, then walked slowly to the drawer in the corner of the room, took out the envelope and opened it. Inside was the equivalent of one hundred pounds in *lire*. Nothing else. No message. The money was replaced in the drawer and Dowson moved back to the door:

'Tidy the room and send up for some food,' he said, and then pointed to the Italian: 'And get that man out of here. He doesn't work for Cinecittà. He's a waiter at Il Cavatappi.'

Dowson then left, closing the door. For a while they heard him in the adjacent room, telephoning, then the main door of the suite closed, leaving the two people in bed, the man pressed against the wall, a gold crucifix around his neck now hanging against his spine, and Antonella with her arm across her breasts, emotionless, her left foot on the carpet resting on one of the Italian's black and red nylon socks.

There are no discrepancies about the events that immediately followed; not the actual events themselves, but the aftermath, for photographs were taken both by the police and the press. They show the interior of a villa on the Appia Antica (a double-page spread in *Oggi* is exceptionally fine and detailed) and more particularly, three ground-floor rooms. According to the account, an intruder had entered the building while the occupant was out, had placed a large lawn sprinkler in the centre of the drawing-room carpet (Persian), as well as in the library (a fine collection of First Folios, some works by Burton and other rare erotica) and the owner's personal study. The three revolving sprinklers had then been turned full on and the visitor had left. It wasn't until the following afternoon when the owner, Baculi, returned with some *fragolini* that the incident was discovered; by which time, of course, despite the fact that the water supply had finally run out, the three rooms belonged to Atlantis.

The caption under one photograph calls the affair 'childish vandalism' and so it must appear. Hence the paradox. Nevertheless, the vandal, childish or not, was never caught.

Eight

Martha Benenden and Emily were the best of friends, and had been ever since they had been at school together. They had become débutantes at the same time and had married their respective husbands within a year of each other (the guest-list was interchangeable) and though for a while, as these things happen, they saw little of each other, their friendship never diminished. In fact quite the reverse. Emily liked Martha because she made her laugh and was practical and organized; she admired the fact that Martha could cope with everything without panicking, could manage Stadshunt, the farm, Rupert, the family (name-tabs and buttons were *never* missing from the clothes of the Benenden sons) with such apparent ease; walking across the fields in gumboots and duffle in winter to feed the horses when her husband was away, always remembering birthdays and replying to invitations, planning outings for the children in the morning and appearing fresh and unruffled at parties in the evening. In this way, she was the total opposite to Emily, who had been known to burst into tears at the breaking of an egg.

On Martha's part, Emily was just Emily, beautiful and fragile, loving and being loved. She was proud when friends praised Stadshunt, its well-kept lawns and flower-beds, the comfort and attention given to guests (those *petits soins* in each bedroom, individually chosen), the good behaviour of the children, but Martha knew she was admired for being a Mother, a Wife, a Hostess, while Emily was loved for just being herself, for simply being a woman men and women alike felt privileged to know and to share an hour or a day with.

At school, Emily had always been everyone's heroine, elusive, the inspiration of the sonnets they were obliged to read. They identified her as Beatrice and Laura and Julia in silks, and younger girls had crushes on her and wanted to be picked to be in her team. Martha never resented this then, nor did she now. She was just proud to have been chosen to be her friend and flattered (though Lady Bowness had been told the reverse) that Emily had asked to stay the weekend at her home.

When the train arrived, Martha was already waiting in the car-park, wearing sweater and jeans, standing by the Land–Rover. She saw Emily immediately and rushed up to the barrier and hugged her and Annabelle, then picked up the suitcase and said that she hadn't been waiting long and isn't the weather absolutely marvellous and that Rupert's gone to a boring horse-fair but would be back in time for dinner.

During the drive back to Stadshunt, Emily spoke very little, merely listening to the anecdotes about the children and the farm and the roses that had died in the kitchen garden. After twenty minutes, the white Victorian house could be seen on the hill, set amid beeches and acacias, and they entered the driveway ('There's my favourite mallard. See? On the edge of the lake. Must think of a name for him.' *'Francis.'* 'Francis?' *'Francis Drake.'* 'Oh, really, Emily, that's *too* much.') and parked at the main door.

Tea was already prepared and waiting, and Annabelle was entrusted to the Benenden nanny and the two women were left alone, sitting in deep armchairs, surrounded by bronze statuettes of horses, flowers in vases, a table behind them with magazines laid out in neat rows as if they were on sale. They talked of friends, cousins, definitely *not* horses, a week-end Martha had spent with one or other of the Royal Family after Goodwood, and though Emily said almost nothing, she didn't regret the visit, for her mind was made up. As she listened to the gossip, she thought she ought to tell Martha about Dowson because there was no one else she could tell, and after two months she just needed to mention his name, to talk to someone she could trust and who would understand. But somehow the occasion didn't arrive and when there was finally an opportunity and the mood was right, Rupert had returned, cursing the car and the horse-fair and offering Emily a drink.

'Telly supper?' he asked and Martha said it was all ready. They had just been waiting for him.

'Well, I'll just do the rounds,' he replied and grinned at Emily and left, slamming the door, a glass of whisky in his hand. They heard him shouting out to the dogs then a side-door opened and closed and there was silence. The moment, however, had gone.

'Obviously he didn't buy any horses.'

'Obviously not.'

On the mantelpiece, Emily could see the postcard she had sent them from Korčula, propped up against a vase. A colour print of the market-place, the gates and the old town beyond. She was surprised it was still there, now that it was almost Whitsun, and she wondered what she had written and how many other mantelpieces, shelves, corners of mirrors still exhibited a record of that second day on the island when she had been alone. *It* is *Mrs Hallam, isn't it?*

When Rupert returned, the television was switched on immediately and they sat, eating omelette and salad on their laps, watching a late-night thriller (*The Big Sleep*) until it finished. During it, Martha glanced at Emily's profile and saw that she wasn't even looking at the screen, the food hardly touched before her. She suggested switching the film off but Rupert refused in outrage as if she had asked him to jump off Niagara.

'*You* want to watch it, don't you, Emily?' he said.

'Yes. Of course … '

'There you are.'

Nevertheless, before it had finished, Emily got up and apologized and said she was tired and ought to go to bed.

'I'm sorry about Rupert,' Martha said as they walked up the stairs. 'But you know he's a television fanatic.'

'That's all right. I'm just tired.'

'Of course. I thought you looked pale.'

They reached the first floor and Martha said:

'Are you sure you want to sleep in the small room? We've made up the guest room especially.'

'No, I know it's a bore, but I'd rather sleep in the small room. It always seems so pretty and cosy. I remember noticing it the last time I was here. The door was open and I remember thinking how attractive it was.'

'All right. I've made the bed up and there's a towel in the cupboard. And I must admit, I rather like the room myself. We usually keep it for single people. Bachelors and that.'

'Well, I *am* single really, aren't I?' said Emily and Martha looked at her then hugged her and drew away shyly and said:

'Did you want … to talk, Emily? I mean, if you're not too tired.'

'No … not now.'

The decision had been made.

Martha then opened the door of the small bedroom and Emily stopped, before entering, and looked at the curtains (oleanders, pink and white), the Morris wallpaper, the bottle of Malvern water by the bedside next to the biographies of whey-faced Queens (Alexandra, Mary, one or other of the Carolines). She heard Martha say:

'By the way, tomorrow an old friend of yours is coming. Couldn't put him off and when he heard *you* were here, it was impossible. You'll see his Rolls, no doubt, in the morning.'

And then the curtains were drawn and Martha left.

Emily undressed slowly, folding her clothes and placing them neatly in a drawer and then put on a long white nightdress with blue bows. After washing her face, cleaning her teeth and brushing her hair, she took the bottle of sleeping tablets from her suitcase and got into bed and filled a tumbler with the Malvern water. She then stared at the pattern of oleanders on the curtains for a long time, then poured all the tablets into her hand, one by one, until the bottle was empty. She placed the first one in her mouth, felt it on her tongue, the hardness, the slight bitter taste and reached for the water.

'Oh—by the way,' Martha interrupted loudly, knocking and entering and holding up two books: 'Just in case you can't sleep. A new Georgette Heyer and an absolutely filthy paperback full of milk-white thighs and heaving buttocks. I read it all in one night and lay back and thought of Queen Victoria,' and Martha giggled then saw the small brown medicine bottle on the coverlet.

'Headache?'

Emily swallowed then felt the tablets hidden in her fist and nodded:

'Just a slight migraine. I get it now and again.'

'How awful. Look, we've got some Panadol somewhere. They're a bit stronger than aspirin.'

'No. I'll be all right. I just need to sleep.'

'Are you sure?'

'Yes. Thank you.'

Martha hesitated, anxious to play the nurse, then said:

'Well, anyway, don't worry about breakfast. Annabelle can eat with Martin and Mrs G. is going to bring egg and bacon up for you on a tray. Coffee or tea?'

'There's no need—'

'No arguments. We don't put out the red carpet for everyone, you know.'

Emily smiled, then turned away, her eyes on the verge of tears.

'Good night, Emily. See you in the morning.'

Martha closed the door quietly and left. The tablets were returned to the bottle, the bottle was placed back in the suitcase and within minutes Emily was asleep, exhausted, waking to the sound of dogs and a car driving up and stopping below her window.

Nine

Two men are sitting in Babington's Tea Rooms in Rome, English muffins and Indian tea, sitting in a panelled corner in silence. A young man in a linen suit, an open-neck silk shirt, his hair long, reclining with one arm resting on the back of an empty chair, as if reluctantly posing for the frontispiece of a slim volume of verse. Opposite him, his back defiantly to the restaurant of cashmere and pearls, an older man is hunched up unshaven, a slight trembling in his movements as he drinks a third cup of coffee, leaving a series of darkening stains on the white table-cloth. They ought to be strangers, for there is nothing to link them either in style, features or character, yet they appeared together and will share the bill. Outside, the Piazza di Spagna is crowded, noisy, a Babylon of tourists in the morning sunlight that now filters through lace curtains, highlighting the specks of dust in the air, the silver teapots, jugs, and the ring on the finger of the young man. There is peace here, refreshing, and though not as English as the proprietors would admit, the restaurant still retains echoes of England, of its past and there is comfort in that.

'I can't do it, Christopher,' Leith said nervously. 'I've tried it before and it's too late.'

'Yes you can,' replied the young man, casually pouring another cup of tea. 'I won't leave you again.'

'That's not enough. I need a drink.'

'Not yet.'

'Don't be a doctor to me, old sport. Look at me. I couldn't even survive another hour.'

Dowson smiled and gazed at a sporting print on a wall

(coach and horses, the Oxford Mail fording a stream) and said:

'I've made plans. For today. You and I.'

'God, I hate Rome,' Leith suddenly murmured and lowered his head to the table. A waitress appeared, eyes narrowed, faces turned, but Dowson ignored them and lit a cigarette and passed it across the table:

'Have a cigarette, then we'll go and visit Keats.'

It was a mistake. They both knew it as soon as they entered the building on the corner of the Spanish Steps. They walked from darkened room to darkened room, were indicated the bed where the poet had died, but there was no longer anything there except a desk where a German tourist was writing a postcard. They both stood on the balcony, trying to visualize a view that had been seen one hundred and fifty years ago but saw only adolescent boys lounging on the Steps, raising an extended hand to the bottom of a passing girl, sniggering in corners.

'This place celebrates his death, not his life.' Dowson shivered.

'Poor sod,' Leith said. 'Poor bloody sod. To die at twenty-five in a Roman bed-sitter, dying alone and believing that he was a tragic failure. Worse, knowing that only a few months, a spring, a single summer could realize his ambitions. But not to be, old sport. What a waste. The boy didn't even have hope.'

'Do you think he thought of England?' Dowson asked, turning back towards the gloom of the interior.

'Every bloody minute. Every damn bloody minute. Look at them,' and Leith gestured to the file of tourists, guide-book in hand, passing through the rooms in cultural apathy, one of them asking where she could buy a belt by Gucci. 'Look at them all. Half of them want to see a corpse, the other half would believe you if you told them Keats was a plumber,' and then he repeated once more: 'Poor sod. What a place to die.'

'Let's go,' said Dowson, taking the actor's arm.

' "O for a draught of vintage, that hath been cooled a long age in the deep delved earth", ' and Leith smiled sadly, turned and they left, pushing through the people and back into the sunlight and the traffic of the Piazza.

Later they visited a bookshop in the Via Cavour and sat and took out all the books on English gardens and houses, placing the large colour-plates before them and turning over the pages silently, pausing at a view of an Adam house, a Tudor wall of roses, a river meandering between green hills in Somerset. They bought an English newspaper just to see the temperature in London, then finally found a small restaurant near the Forum and took a table on the cobblestones beneath vines.

'Let's have some wine now,' Dowson said and ordered a carafe. 'I need it as much as you.'

They ate sparingly, feeling very close to each other, all thoughts of the film and Baculi forgotten. They were grateful for each other's company, but pensive, their minds preoccupied with the experience of the morning. Finally Leith said, hesitantly, but with affection:

'Christopher ... tell me it's none of my business —'

'It's none of your business.'

'All right, but why have you never talked about Emily since we left Korčula? You don't have to say anything, but — oh, for God's sake, old sport, you can't just dismiss her like that. You hurt that woman, you know. You hurt her.'

There was a pause, then Dowson nodded:

'I know.'

'Then what are you running away from? I'm not blind, old sport. I know what you feel about her. Go back to England and see her, or at least write to her.'

'All right,' Dowson shrugged, 'I am running away. But that is my choice, Leith, not yours.'

'But running away from what!' Leith shouted in despair. 'No man in his right senses would run away from Emily. And don't tell me it's from England, because what have we been doing all day? We haven't been walking around Rome, old sport. We've been walking around England. Every bloody minute.'

Dowson didn't answer, almost as if he hadn't heard, as if Leith was talking to someone at another table. He merely gestured to the waiter and ordered coffee.

'And a large brandy for me,' added Leith defiantly. 'Let's *both* behave like children.'

There was a long silence, then Dowson looked at the actor, then at the square, a small water-fountain set into a wall, a sheet placed over a balcony of a house opposite.

'When I was in Florence ... ' he began, then stopped and didn't say any more. The coffee and the brandy were brought and drunk and Leith realized that Dowson was no longer with him. Physically, yes, sitting in profile across the table, but he knew that nothing else around him existed. The conversation was still-born, the mask had reappeared. Dowson, as ever, had assumed the enigma.

*   *   *

He was the only child, born in London a year before the War, when his father finally returned to England from Egypt. A terraced-square background where he stayed for his first year, and then when his father went back once more to the African Desert, six years in Yorkshire, living with his mother in a manor in the West Riding; then returning at last to the same square and the same house amid the rubble.

There are one or two photographs of Dowson as a child

(a snapshot of himself and his mother in Margate) but little else to record the first decade of his life. The house where he was born is no longer there and there are no letters. I have photostats of three school reports that show him to be intelligent and artistic, as well as rebellious. What form the rebellion took I am not sure, but his lack of attendance was criticized repeatedly and it appears he was often punished. The only teacher who replied to my letters (once again we are confronted by that tacit refusal to talk) taught him when he was fourteen and in the brief note — four lines, apart from the acknowledgment — described Dowson as 'silent, solitary and unapproachable'. That, alone, is consistent.

It is not the adolescence, however, that concerns me — partly because too much of it is conflicting and unreliable, and partly because it would be too easy to draw Freudian conclusions, amateur assumptions, and that, mercifully, is not my *forte*. What *do* concern me are the years, months even, before he met Emily, and one would think the facts and details would be mountainous. After all, we are thinking of events that happened barely five years ago at the most, where even a hermit or a monk could not exist without being remembered by someone. Consequently, in preparing this book, I anticipated volumes of anecdotes, memories, friends and enemies prepared to reminisce, but there is almost nothing. A mere scrap, a timetable of irrelevant events (he was known to be here, it was heard that he was living there) but little else. In frustration I even considered that he may well have been in prison, but records prove this to be false, as I suspected. It is almost as if Christopher Dowson didn't exist (despite his birth certificate in Somerset House), as if he appeared for the first time at Stadshunt in that November of 1967 from an alien planet. But he did exist, did have a child-hood and a maturity, like you and me, even if there is little evidence to prove it. *Silent, solitary and unapproachable*. The phrase perhaps says all that need be told.

And yet there is more, an affair that I learnt about by chance, just as I was about to abandon my research altogether. It is obvious that Dowson had to live somewhere (and it is reasonable to conclude that most of the time it was not in England, or at least in London); it is also obvious that he had to earn money somehow, simply to eat. From what has already been written, it can be seen that he was not unresourceful in such a field, and though I would hesitate to accuse him of existing by illegal means, he can certainly be called amoral. This is not a judgment, nor even a criticism, but simply a fact. It may not explain much about his past, but it does shed light on his character.

Even if one discounts Abel-Hardy's story about Dowson in Biarritz, there is enough evidence elsewhere to convince me that Dowson was attracted by—and indeed very attractive to—the rich, and more particularly, what is termed 'the idle rich'. Members of this particular species I know very well, have seen them and been with them, in Marbella and Cannes, in Marrakesh, Sardinia and St Moritz and a dozen other places. I have attended their miserable soirées in Venice and Bavaria, their country weekends in Berkshire and Martha's Vineyard and stayed on their vulgar yachts in Portofino; indeed I am on nodding terms with the whole social register from the Aga Khan to the shipowner's wife. I am, in short, idle and rich myself. Or at least I was until I tried to beat the Greek Syndicate at their own game.

Be that as it may, at the time Dowson was in Rome with Leith, I was in a club in Curzon Street, which is where I first learnt about Dowson and a girl whom I will refer to as Celia Batleigh.

I was playing roulette with Emily's brother, using the Martingale system, and, much to my surprise and the aggravation of the *chef*'s ulcer, was winning extensively. On my right, also on a good streak, was a Swiss-German millionaire, very handsome though wretchedly vain (you have seen his face many times in the tabloids, I am sure) who had just divorced his wife, a sensual international beauty whom I had seen many times, either in a bikini or out of it. Anyway, as the game progressed, I could hear the conversation between the millionaire and an English interior decorator who was a fellow member of Boodles. I can't recall the gist of the discussion (remember I am *en plein* on 23) but suddenly, quite clearly and quite distinctly, I heard the name 'Dowson'. There was no doubt about that. Of course, it is not such an uncommon name but I was as sure as Martingale was about his system, that they were talking about Christopher Dowson.

I waited till the interior decorator (Ludstone) had left the table (just in time, may I add, for the roulette tide had turned) and hurried to him before he left:

'Ludstone — don't think I'm drunk, but did you mention someone called Dowson? Just now. At the table?'

He looked at me as if I were insane. We both loathed each other and knew it (I couldn't stand his hair, and he just couldn't stand me on any terms) and so he wondered why on earth I was talking to him.

'Dowson?' I repeated. 'Did you mean *Christopher* Dowson?'

A blonde girl (model, kind to animals) moved forward and put her arm on Ludstone's shoulder.

'Do you know this Dowson then?' he said.

'No. But I met him at Stadshunt. Young, dark, half-Greek —'

'Look, dear chap, I don't know why you're so interested, because frankly I've never even seen him.'

'But you mentioned his name.'

'Only because he used to go out with Celia Batleigh. If you have to eavesdrop, eavesdrop properly.'

He then began to move away, his arm around the girl.

'Celia Batleigh?' I said. 'I don't know her. Where's she live?'

'She doesn't live anywhere. She's dead. Died last October. Good God, where *have* you been?'

'I'm sorry ... but Dowson—Dowson knew her, you said.'

'She told me she had an affair with someone called Dowson if that's what you mean.'

'I see ... '

'Do you? Well, if you meet him again, ask him why he didn't go to the bloody funeral.'

*   *   *

'Hats. I remember the hats, the canvases on the wall, the brass bed found in a market, the collage of popular idols on one wall, a painting by Boshier, a photograph of James Dean. The coffee mugs, the house, the room, the coloured hats, a painting of Marilyn Monroe, paper flowers, trinkets, the nights in bed, the dances at the art college on Friday evenings. The solitude of both our existences in that Victorian room, knowing none of her friends, she knowing none of mine, the smile, the blonde hair, Ravel and Buddy Holly on a record player on the stripped-board floor. Hats and dresses and jeans. The first "love you" then "I love you" then "I am in love with you", loving, the brittleness of the happiness, her nakedness, the childhood toys, enthusiasms, the rare moment of weeping. The departure inevitably, the bursting of the comet, separating for reasons I will never know. The hats ...

'Then the absence, the long summers, glimpsing her in a Saturday pub, laughing across the saloon yard through alien faces, through her friends whom I never knew and who never knew me. I had been introduced once but they had forgotten, possessing her happiness like a fragile doll, fencing the light, the radiance. The loving.

'And I remember the October. I was in a train, in a fast train to Scotland and had bought a newspaper. I hadn't seen her for two years, not really seen her and I saw her name. It was a small paragraph on the third page, I almost overlooked it, a small paragraph and her name. It said that she had died of cancer and that the funeral was that day. And I didn't even know. Didn't even know about the illness, didn't even know anything and I was in this train, this carriage, there are no corridors and the next stop is two hours away and I will be in Doncaster and she was being buried in — Just a short paragraph, no more than four lines. I never knew and I am in a carriage, sealed, being drawn away. Helpless. Utterly, totally helpless.

'Hats, the nakedness, the loving. Celia, help me.'

Silence. Leith closed the exercise book (a child's red exercise book, margin and lines) and gazed out of the window of the hotel. After a while, he heard Dowson in the corridor approaching and he quickly replaced the book in the suitcase where he had found it.

Dowson entered, grinning, looking happy, and pointed joyfully to the bottle of vodka on the table.

'You've done it! You've hardly touched a drop. I *told* you you could do it.'

And then Dowson laughed and hugged Leith and then dropped on to the sofa and stared at the ceiling, relaxed.

'God, it's hot,' he said.

Leith didn't move, keeping his back to the sofa then he sat down.

'Christopher ... Let's get out of Rome. We both hate it. I couldn't give a damn about filming any more. Let's take the yacht and leave.'

An arm was raised in casual agreement:

'Whatever you say. Where do you want to go? Africa?

The Caribbean? India? No — not India. Hong Kong. Tell me where you want to go and I will follow.'

Leith looked at Dowson, a pause, then he said:

'England ... You remember England, don't you, old sport?'

Ten

I arrived at Stadshunt, as I planned, in time for breakfast, that Portia's party-piece of covered dishes that could reveal anything from kedgeree to cold-baked eggs. Rupert was already at the table reading *Horse and Hound* (inevitably) and acknowledged my presence with an idle gesture towards the hot-plate and an apology for the coffee. He should have apologized for both, for the food was abysmal (someone, someday, should write a novella on the gastronomic myopia of the aristocracy) and so I contented myself with a self-made cup of tea and the gossip columns, and waited for Emily to appear. With the best will in the world, I avoided all conversations, on the theory that no one, but no one, should be either witty or conscious at the breakfast-table. I was grateful, therefore, when Emily finally did arrive, descending the staircase, looking pale and enchanting. Beautiful women, I am convinced, should always be first seen descending staircases (preferably Georgian with a touch of Grinling Gibbons), descending with the light decorating the hair, eyes lowered, nakedness restricted only to the feet and perhaps the left ankle.

We exchanged greetings and she took my hand and said that she was happy to see me and did I really drive all the way from London.

'Of course not. Denbigh drove,' I replied. 'I merely sat in the back and waved out of the window.'

I noticed her eyes once more (the image recurring yet again) and suspected that she had been crying. Not recently but within the past few hours, for there was a reddish hue beneath the eyelashes, a disguised puffiness that I had rarely seen before. It was the first time I had met her since my last visit to Stadshunt and there was no doubt that she had changed. Thinner perhaps, the bone structure in her face finer, the hair not quite so well groomed, a slight hesitation in her actions, a distance, but at the time I could only attribute this to Hallam, for remember, Dowson as yet meant nothing to me.

When Martha arrived, red cheeks, wellingtons, a pair of pruning shears in her hand, it was suggested that swimming should be the plan for the morning. It was hot, Rupert's mother, Lady Benenden (an awesome woman who wore hats day and night and spoke as if she were addressing an annual convention for the deaf), possessed a swimming-pool in the shape of someone's liver, set amid lawns and roses and a child's swing tied to a tree.

'But I haven't got a costume,' said Emily in a shy attempt at avoiding the issue.

'Then borrow one of mine!' shouted Rupert, laughing. 'Go topless! It's all the rage.'

'I have a spare bikini,' said Martha, with a glare at her husband Medusa would have been proud of. 'That's if you want to go.'

'Well ... if you are *all* going ... '

'Of course she is. Aren't you, Emily?' interrupted Rupert and put his arm around her waist.

There was a pause, Martha glanced at me then at Emily then nodded:

'We'll take Annabelle and Martin and go in two cars.'

'There's no need,' I said. 'We can all squeeze into mine.'

'You haven't still got that ten-ton truck have you?' Rupert asked, glancing under the lids of all the breakfast dishes.

'I'm afraid so.'

'Bloody great thing. Where can you park a thing like that?'

116

'In your driveway. Besides, there's little *else* I have to show the world.'

A child, whom I recognized as Emily's youngest daughter, appeared and ran up to her mother and clung to her legs, hiding her face. For a brief moment adult and child were frozen, a single unit, Emily's face lowered in profile, one hand resting on Annabelle's head, identical hair, white-gold, a Victorian water-colour.

'Do *you* want to go swimming, Annabelle?'

The child's head moved. Yes.

And so it was agreed.

If I hadn't loved Emily Hallam before, been in love with her when she was Emily Bowness, it would have happened that weekend in June. I knew that I could never attain her (that was realized long ago) or even be loved by her from a distance, but I believed I was her friend and I am grateful for that. If one has to quote Proust, and I see no reason at the moment why one shouldn't, it would be this: *There is nothing like desire for preventing the things we say from having any resemblance to the things in our minds.* It isn't the best he has to offer, but I remembered the phrase that day as we approached Lady Benenden's house and consequently resolved to say as little as possible, and simply observe. I had seen something in Emily's face at breakfast, in her eyes, that disturbed me, for having known her for over ten years, it was alien to her character. I cannot describe it exactly, no words were said, but I knew that she was harbouring a great secret, a secret that was slowly destroying her from within, like a tooth decaying unperceived except to the x-ray. At one moment, just as we were entering the car, she looked at me (I was wearing an off-white linen suit in celebration of the season) and there was a sudden plea for help, she touched my sleeve, then the moment was gone and the morning dissolved slowly into laughter.

117

Perhaps it was the champagne, the absence of Rupert's mother who had generously deserted us for a regatta, or just the peace of four friends sitting in an English garden on a warm summer's day. But I remember noticing the happiness suddenly appearing within Emily, as if she had been reborn, giggling like a schoolgirl with Martha as they appeared from the house in hideous bikinis that were modest enough for my mother. I watched her swimming, diving from the edge of the pool, a Seurat abstract of pink and green under the water, then surfacing, laughing, her hair smearing her forehead before descending under the water once more.

Then the shouts, the splashing, Rupert attempting an embarrassed grab for Martha's bikini top, the emphatic gestures for me to join them (not on your life), the pushing and ducking and finally the gasped sighs as the three of them collapsed on to the lawn and lay still, recovering their breath, allowing the sun to dry them while the children paddled.

'Anyone got any cigarettes?'

'Under the tree.'

'God, it's hot.'

'Which tree?'

'The tree in front of you. Tall thing with leaves on it.'

'Annabelle — stay on the steps.'

'There *are* no cigarettes under the tree.'

'Of course there are. I can see them from here.'

'Anyone want more champagne?'

'Yes *please*!'

'Is it still cold?'

'Oh, Rupert, don't be so bloody fussy.'

'I'm not being fussy. Champagne should be drunk cold. Just as tea should be drunk hot.'

'I *like* cold tea.'

'Oh for heaven's sake, just throw over the bloody ciggies.'

'It's empty.'

'What is?'

'The packet. It's empty.'

'Oh, hell. I might as well just go to sleep.'

During this, I observed Emily as I had previously resolved. She was lying face down on the grass about ten yards from me, her arms parallel to her body, watching her daughter at the shallow end of the pool. A lazy curve from head to toe, the water still glistening on the skin of her back and legs, her hand suddenly scratching a shoulder, a brief look at me and a smile as Martha searched for the cigarettes, then turning away. Roses, the sound of bees, the heat hovers. After a while, when Rupert was asleep and Martha in despair had returned to the pool, I walked across to her and sat down.

'You're not brown at all?'

'What?'

'Brown. You're not brown at all,' I said. 'I thought you would have a deep sun-tan.'

'Well, it was raining in Cumberland most of the time.'

'I mean in Korčula. I got your card and you said it was boiling. I expected you to look like a coffee bean. Not the shape. The colour.'

There was a silence, then she moved her head slightly, moved aside a fringe of wet hair, and looked up at me and said quite simply:

'I kept in the shade.'

'Did you like it? Korčula?'

'Very much.'

'Then you must tell me all about it. I've never been there.'

Emily didn't reply for a moment, looking at the grass, then said:

'One day I will. I promise you.'

And that really was that. I didn't pursue the matter, nor in fact did I need to. For by the next day I knew everything there was to know, and the first pieces of this jigsaw that is before you now began to be assembled.

*   *   *

In the afternoon, after leaving the children to rest at Stadshunt, we went to visit a friend of mine who had been captain of my house at Eton and had inherited not only a castle and more titles than are on a library shelf, but a family tree that went back to Gog and Magog. The castle, which you may well have visited, was on the Avon, and on a map of Warwickshire had occupied its share of acreage since the Plantagenets — the Nevilles had once tethered their horses in the courtyard and eaten in the scullery and it is reported that the Duke of Clarence himself had once lodged in the East Tower (now, like Clarence, no longer there) drinking malmsey wine, a particular penchant. As the years passed, however, and the accents of successive monarchs ceased to be English or even intelligible, the boundaries of the Russelton land diminished, gradually at first through tax, debt or amnesia, then more rapidly as one owner, Thomas, the seventeenth Earl, a temperate rake, gambled away the view from the armoury window in a single game of faro. The recipient (later blackballed from White's) took possession of his claim the next day and turned it into a private fox-hunt, after first, of course, cutting down the body of Thomas from one of the peach trees (badly in need of pruning).

The castle is still habitable, though except for the required ration of servants, there is only Russelton himself, still a bachelor and heterosexual (at least his dowager mother hopes so), living alone in one corner of the building amid the Holbeins and the catherine-wheels of muskets and pikes and the ghosts of his ancestors.

When we arrived, he was in his study, sitting before a table, upon which were about a dozen packets of flower seeds, as if he were inventing an eccentric game of patience. Emily was the first to be kissed on the cheek (she being yet another distant cousin), then we all had tea and talked about the merits of linoleum for reasons that are quite beyond me. Afterwards, Russelton suddenly got up, his face pink with excitement, and declared that he had something simply extraordinary and marvellous that he had bought for the castle and that we all must see it immediately.

'But what is it?' asked Martha.

'Wait and see,' replied Russelton, giggling with the pride of someone who had just invented the jet engine.

In a castle in which the paintings in the Great Hall alone outrivalled the Tate Gallery, and where the silver could pay off the National Debt, we all expected anything and everything and so followed, hardly breathing a word, through corridors containing exquisite beauty (tapestries from Aubusson, furniture by Hepplewhite, knick-knacks by Fabergé and Nicholas Hilliard), past portraits of monarchs and mistresses, landscapes, jewels, dresses, the gloves of a beheaded queen, hurrying past them all in the wake of this White Rabbit ahead of us, who scurried through the fragile treasures of history as if they were tins of beans in a local supermarket.

'Do you know where we're going?' I heard Martha whisper and Emily shook her head and both women spontaneously began to suppress giggles and once had to stop in a corner, handkerchiefs stuffed in their mouth, shoulders shaking, pretending to admire a halberd.

We were soon descending steps towards the dungeons (a cell where a saint had lived contained a boiler), along another corridor that had recently been painted. It was soon evident that we were in an area that had been converted into the visitors' canteen. A door was opened, and the twentieth Earl of Russelton stepped aside and pointed:

'There!'

We all looked in puzzlement, then at each other, then the prized acquisition was indicated once again. It was a transparent plastic ball, the size of a desk globe, for cooling and containing soft drinks; a simple sphere half full of liquid within which a plastic orange bounced up and down ceaselessly on the surface.

'Isn't it exquisite? The visitors adore it. Don't you think it's the most marvellous thing you've ever seen?'

There are moments like this, too rare perhaps, when one's faith in the future of mankind is boundless.

'I think he's insane. He's bloody insane. A castle crammed with the most priceless objects in the world and he shows us a fucking plastic orange.'

We are in the Rolls. Emily is sitting opposite me, Rupert shouting on my left, Martha in hysterics almost on the floor.

'God help us all. A fucking plastic bloody orange!'

Emily smiled then began to laugh and the laughter became infectious until tears were running down our cheeks and instinctively, as I was sitting on the fold-up seat, I clutched Emily to steady myself and suddenly felt her tremble and then tense and break away. The action was a mere fraction of a second, nothing more, noticed by no one, for Emily continued laughing, though the spontaneity had gone.

'Fifty Elizabethan miniatures,' continued Rupert, 'ten rooms of First Folios, God knows how many Reynolds and Turners and Constables, and he shows us a plastic bouncing fucking orange.'

That night, as I learnt the next day, Emily told Martha about Dowson. She waited till she had gone to her room and then she told her, both women sitting in nightdresses on the bed with mugs of chocolate, the door locked. The light, I understand, wasn't switched off till four in the morning.

Eleven

'But what did you tell her?'

'Well—what *could* I say? I knew something was wrong but I never expected *that*.'

'And you're sure it was Dowson?'

'Yes. I told you.'

'The same Dowson who—'

'Yes! But it doesn't matter who it is—she's in love with him.'

'The bastard. I never thought he'd be like that.'

'Poor Emily. It was awful. She was just in tears all the time. Doesn't know where he is. Nothing. Left without a word.'

'The bastard.'

'It's all very well to keep calling him a bastard but what on earth are we going to do?'

It is Sunday and Martha and I are walking across the fields in no particular direction, walking towards the hills with the sound of church bells in the distance. A clear sky, the light bright, a cluster of crows suddenly scattering from an oak tree to our left. A man in a near-by field waving to us and pointing up at a hawk.

'You haven't told Rupert, have you?'

'Good God, no,' replied Martha. 'He still hasn't forgiven him for turning up before from nowhere. His solution would be to get an elephant gun and hunt him down.'

'Well, it's one answer.'

'You keep forgetting she's in *love* with him. She said … she said she had never loved anyone, not even Edward at the beginning, as much as she loves Christopher Dowson. She's just empty—that's what she said—totally empty. Do you know she almost tried to commit suicide?'

'What? I don't believe it. When?'

'Friday night. She didn't of course, because of the children or something but—oh, it's so awful. Emily of all people. Anyone, *anyone*, but her.'

'Do you think she'd try it again? I mean—suicide?'

'No. I asked her that.'

'The bastard. What a bastard.'

'Oh, stop going on about *him*. Think about *her*!'

There *are* no solutions of course. There are the usual clichés, toe-holds back to some kind of stability such as Time Heals All Things, Other Fish in the Sea, Life Must Go On, and all the rest of those kindergarten platitudes we propound out of helplessness. There are the gestures of comfort that suffocate, the reassurances that we all 'understand', the vain assumptions that everything will be 'all right', that he would return, that he had lost her address and other such pitiful remarks, but they are all, in the end, futile. We, the observers of someone else's unhappiness, even with the best intentions in the world, are irritated by it, selfish as that may sound; we want it to go away, want a simple equation to solve everything, like bandage and ointment on a scratch. We want to shoulder the responsibility on to someone else (a doctor, a priest, there are people after all, dear, who are professionally qualified for such things) no matter how much we love the victim before us. At first we try self-consciously to soothe the pain, but not for long. We are human, we haven't the time, we resent someone suddenly being different from what they were. We are helpless. And deep down, we know that whatever we may do to lessen the despair, the person before us is alone, will sleep and suffer alone, and if it is someone we love, we are all cowards at heart. It is too easy to help a stranger in distress, assisting a drunk in the street, a car

casualty, a remote acquaintance, for there is a smug satisfaction in that, whether we admit it or not. The Good
Samaritan never did deserve *all* the medals we keep pinning
to his burnous. But for someone we love, someone close to
us, like Emily, there are, I repeat, no solutions. None at all.

'We'd better get back,' Martha said. 'I don't want to leave
her alone.'

'Do you want her to stay at Stadshunt?'

'Yes, but I don't think she should. I mean she's sleeping
in Dowson's room, where he was. And there's Rupert and
the children—oh, I'm not trying to—'

'I know. I'll take her back to London. She can stay in her
brother's flat. He won't be there, will he?'

'Antony? No, he's leaving tomorrow, she said. But do you
think it's the right thing?'

'I have no idea. But perhaps if we surround her with
people, with friends, she might ... well, not feel so alone.'

'*You* ask her then, won't you? She trusts you.'

I looked at Martha and was about to reply when we saw
Rupert approaching, carrying an empty bran bucket.

'Come on, you two. I've been looking for you. Where
have you been?'

'Admiring your estate,' I replied.

'Well, come on back to the house. I've decided to chal-
lenge Emily to a game of table-tennis. Sixpence a game. Any
side-bets?'

'No, Rupert,' I said. 'I'm sure you'll win.'

✳   ✳   ✳

There was little persuasion needed. Now that Emily had
unburdened her heart to Martha, she felt embarrassed being
in the same house, as if she were an intruder. Perhaps, like
drunks and Catholics, one should always reveal one's soul
only to strangers, for she became conscious of every action,

every consideration taken by her girl friend, and was guilty for that. It seemed to her as if she had no right to disrupt the traditional routine of Stadshunt, and though talking of Dowson had brought some relief, she now wanted to leave, to avoid the pity she felt on entering a room, the oblique asides glimpsed from the corner of her eye. And so she accepted my invitation to travel to London, kissed Martha goodbye and left while Rupert was out riding.

In the car, Annabelle sat next to Denbigh (paper and crayons on her lap) before the partition, while Emily and I sat in the back, the Sunday papers at our feet, not speaking for a while as the Rolls made its way via Oxford towards London.

'Do you want to listen to music?' I asked. 'Very orthodox. All the popular classics or Stan Getz, or there's something I rather like by someone called Harry Nilsson.'

'No, thank you. Not now ... '

'Well, we could always read the advertisements in the supplements or play pub-signs. Count the legs, that kind of thing.'

Emily smiled but didn't reply and gazed out of the window at the streets and houses of Banbury, at a bus that had stopped beside us at some traffic lights. Why do people always stare into the back of a Rolls Royce with a mixture of envy and then acute resentment when they realize you are neither the Queen of England nor Dracula?

'Shall I tell you a story about someone I met?'

'Is it happy, sad or totally untrue?' Emily asked.

'All three. His name was Xysto — with an X — and when he was introduced to people he was always flattered to discover that his phone number was eagerly demanded, because he was the most unattractive creature you'd ever hope to see. That's the happy part. The sad part is that in time Xysto learnt that his name was merely used to occupy a blank page in an address book for his telephone never rang.'

Emily nodded and looked at me, then turned away, and lit a cigarette. Behind the partition Annabelle was holding up a page of blue scribble.

I remember little else about the journey, or at least there is little to recall, for few words were exchanged. I had resolved to tell Emily that I knew about Dowson and this I did. Surprisingly there was little reaction, as if she was aware that Martha had talked to me (after all, we had been seen together for two hours both by Emily and Rupert). I assured her that no one else would know but she seemed apathetic about that, as if it didn't really matter any more. She was proud certainly, as we all are in such matters, but I am sure she felt no regrets and was perhaps slowly cancelling the experience, Dowson, Korčula, out of her mind. It was of course impossible but I suspected that she was prepared to try. I therefore didn't pursue the subject and we talked about, oh, irrelevancies, allowing the journey to dictate the conversation. For example, as we passed through Oxford where I had spent three miserable years before being sent down (or up, in my case, since I was living in Derbyshire) she pointed to some snoozing spires on our right and said:

'Isn't that your college?'

'That one? Yes.'

'James was there at the same time, wasn't he?'

'Your brother? Yes, but in another year. Do you realize he took my room at Folly Bridge when I left? Quite a prized possession.'

'Yes, I remember seeing him there.'

'At Folly Bridge?'

'Yes.'

'What's he doing now?' I asked. 'Is he still with Christie's?'

'No. Said he saw so many awful paintings being brought in to be assessed that he decided to paint some himself.'

'And did he?'

'Not a single one.'

'Well, as long as you don't, no one will ever suspect that you can't.'

Then silence and we both studied the back of Denbigh's head until we entered the suburbs of Slough.

'Have you any plans?' I asked, glancing at Emily.

'You mean while I am in London?'

'While you're in London.'

She stared ahead of her, eyes slightly narrowed, and it was the profile of the Gibson Girl. I'd never noticed that similarity before but if you have seen those sensitive pen-drawings, usually bound in large folios, collections of Charles Dana Gibson's drawings of a wistful Edwardian beauty in sleeveless dresses, chin tilted, and usually seen reclining on a chaise-longue vainly awaiting a billet-doux, or simply gazing out of the picture at the viewer, the long line of the neck amid draperies, then you will understand what I mean. The sketches had always been favourites of mine and I suppose in a way it was because I saw Emily within them (despite Gibson's heroine being brunette) though I hadn't realized it till this moment. It's a scant basis for a digression but I am waiting for Emily to reply, and am almost convinced after a while that she will not. But finally she smiled slightly, a mere suggestion at the corners of her mouth, then leaned back in the seat, her mind resolved.

'Do you realize,' she said, staring into space, speaking quietly and carefully, 'that I haven't lived as a single girl since I was sixteen? I mean been *accepted* as such by friends, you, everyone? I've always been the mother or the wife for over ten years, and now I'm twenty-seven years old and I suppose it's time I began before it's too late.'

'Unlike Xysto, the telephone will never stop ringing,' I said.

She considered that, then looked at me:

'It's really quite terrifying, isn't it? I mean I *am* single in a way, and there's no alternative. I refuse to be a recluse and for a while, at home, I almost became one. Like a hedgehog in hibernation … I wanted to become a child again, to be tucked up in bed and told to clean my teeth.'

Then she smiled briefly, a slight blush on her cheeks and she concentrated on lighting another cigarette, her hand shaking slightly.

'I'd have to get a nanny for Annabelle.'

'That wouldn't be too difficult.'

A pause. We are passing the airport, moving fast on the motorway.

'The trouble is — how do I begin?'

'Well, I'll contact a staff agency for you in the morning —'

'No, I mean — in London. I would have to buy dresses, clothes, almost everything. And what about my hair — it's much too long —'

I remember Emily then stopped, with almost a look of fear in her eyes, then smiled and said without emotion:

'If only … '

The next day, Emily and I re-entered London Society, whatever *that* may be. For the first three weeks, we were seen at parties, private views, dinners, Sunday lunches, gala openings (and closings) and all the inane trivia that makes up the cultural swamp of London west of the Park — Islington and Barnes, of course, justifiably avoided like the plague. We followed the lemmings of actors and writers and bored second sons of peers and producers and bad-tempered poets; sat on large cushions dressed in clothes from Blades and Thea Porter and drank and smoked and carefully assumed the air of bored impertinence so essential for being accepted. We allowed ourselves to be adopted and pigeon-holed and did our damnedest to be ill enough to visit that lovely doctor in Ebury Street. The circles of acquaintances spread, linking each other (Daring Theatrical Set, Cheque-book Gypsy Set, Chester Square American Set, and of course that life and soul of every parlour, the Gucci-shoed Revolutionary), over-lapping in all their urbane monotony.

Men soon began to flirt with Emily, sitting at her feet, extolling Marx while they finished the host's whisky and scrambled to be invited to ducal weekends, or grinned at her across a stripped-pine table like a stoned hyena and phoned her up in the early hours of the morning. Everything, inevitably, revolved around her and she began to laugh, enjoying the puerile façade of it all, aware of it yet submitting to it because it was new, because she felt liberated, and wore beautiful dresses in zaffre and gold and gave the pretence of being happy. And in a way, I believe she was for a while until everything seemed a mere repetition. There *were* close friends (many in fact) whom she visited and went shopping with and listened to their stories of unhappy affairs with someone in Wales, or of husbands who had been seen with gossip-column hostesses; and there were occasions (a ballet, a dinner party, a boat trip along the Thames) when she felt everything wasn't *all* superficial. She was flattered by every-one and she enjoyed it because she needed to be; she was asked advice and she gave it and she began to enjoy the company of individual men, though there were no affairs.

And as it became July, she eagerly planned summer holidays with varying groups of people—a caravan outing to Scotland, a villa in Spain, a visit to Ireland—and looked forward to them, sitting in her flat with maps and guests lying near her on the floor, the television mute. I myself accompanied her often, despite my natural aversion to Kensington capers, playing the role of charming eunuch well, and dined with her and took her to a premiere (*one* film premiere is more than enough for any sane man's lifetime) and we would take tea at the Ritz and buy books in Hatchards and visit friends in the country for weekends. Such things were far from being novelties for either of us, but to Emily they *appeared* new, a rejuvenation, and I believe, as the days and weeks passed, that Dowson was forgotten, not completely, for that was impossible, but he had entered the category of nostalgia, to be recollected in a brief silence, a scrapbook taken from an attic trunk. For on the surface, Emily seemed happy, had again become the cynosure she had always been and her energy seemed tireless.

July (wet as ever) became August, and Emily bought a car, a Mini, and she would go for drives with the children, myself with Annabelle on my lap, and we decided to visit all the historical buildings in London that the whole world had seen except the Londoner himself. The Tower was mercifully understanding and there was a certain fascination in St Paul's (Wellington's funeral carriage alone is worth the bus-fare) and Hampton Court. There, I recall, as we were walking through the corridor containing the portraits of the Windsor Beauties (they might be beauties in Windsor but in Hampton Court there's a struggle) I turned to Emily and asked her if she was pleased that she came to London. There was no hesitation:

'Yes. Not that I normally enjoy the life and the people here, but I *am* pleased. I realize everything is, or was, a distraction, but I feel stronger now and happier.'

'And—'

'Christopher? You see, I mention his name without a stammer. I have accepted that I will never see him again and that really is the most important achievement, isn't it? The acceptance.'

'Yes.'

'It would have been worse if I had been like them,' and she gestured to the row of mistresses of Charles the Second, lined up along one wall. 'To be discarded and having to live every day in court within the man's sight, seeing him with someone else. At least I am spared that.'

'Well, I wouldn't pity them too much. They were all made Duchesses or whatever. That one over there in the yellow dress and the face of a cod even got her ample body on the back of a penny.'

'Small consolation when she really wanted her head under a crown,' and Emily laughed and we planned to visit the Opera that very evening, something we hadn't done for ages.

'It's all like one enormous holiday,' Emily said as we drove back to London. 'I know it won't last but it really *is* a holiday to me.'

There was one small incident, however, that same day in fact, that I can also repeat. We returned to her apartment building to discover the porter waiting for us in the hall with a telegram for Emily. As he handed it to her, I remember saying: 'Unlike everyone else, I adore telegrams. Always hope they're going to tell me that a rich uncle has died and left me his estate plus two beagles.'

Emily smiled and opened the envelope and read it then turned away, very still, her face white.

'Anything wrong?' I asked.

She turned, she turned away, she turned to the porter, then to the lift, not knowing where to look, thrusting the telegram in my hand, taking it back, returning it, then stood stock-still, frozen.

I looked at the piece of paper in my hand and I must admit it meant nothing to me whatsoever. There was no name, no identification of the sender, merely a time, place and date of a cremation and a four-word message. I repeat, the telegram meant nothing to me then, but I assumed it must have had some significance because that evening I went to the Opera alone. All I realized was that whoever *Old Sport* might be, he was dead.

Twelve

Dowson was already in the ante-room, alone, standing and staring out across the gravel yard and the car-park. He didn't appear to be waiting for anything, merely passing the time of day, someone who had simply wandered by the building by chance and had decided to see what it looked like from the inside. He was still sun-tanned, his hair longer, dressed in a dark corduroy suit and wearing a regimental tie, blue and gold stripes.

When Emily arrived (grey coat, darker hat, her face pale) he didn't look at her immediately, though he had seen her taxi arrive and was aware of her presence in the small, white-painted room. Nor did he speak, for there was little either of them could say at a time like this. A mere silent individuality, two people involved in their own thoughts, that numbing of the mind and body that acts as a merciful anaesthetic, a man standing staring out of a window, a woman sitting down and taking a cigarette from her bag and discovering that she has no matches, hesitating then saying:

'Do you have a light? I've forgotten ... '

Dowson turned and looked at her, then nodded and walked slowly towards her and lit the cigarette.

'There's a smudge,' he said.

'Where?'

'On your cheek. Just there.'

Emily placed a handkerchief to her cheek and moved it slightly across her face.

'Has it gone?'

'Let me see? Yes.'

It was ten minutes past twelve by a clock on the wall,

though that may well have been inaccurate for there seemed no sign of activity from the red-brick building opposite. Other peoples' chauffeurs were still there, an organ could be heard.

'May I sit down next to you?' Dowson asked, and Emily nodded, almost as if they were strangers meeting for the first time, as if nothing had ever happened. She felt nervous; they had slept together, made love, *admitted* their love, and yet it seemed an impertinence to even touch his sleeve.

'Just you and I,' Dowson said, very quietly. 'You asked me in Korčula if he had any friends and I said *we* were his friends. I never realized how pathetically true that was. No one else here. Not even his wife.'

'I read about it in the papers. It didn't seem like the same man. What they said.'

'He just said he wanted to lie down. We had only been in Suffolk a week. He said he felt tired and wanted to lie down. And then he died.'

'I wish I had been there ... '

'In the morning, in the hotel, a woman was in the lobby. A small woman with a brown coat. Forty, forty-five. She was with her husband and she asked him who had died last night. She didn't know but she had heard something. She was standing by the desk, the reception desk, and she asked her husband who had died and he said: "I don't know. Some actor." That's all he said. Some actor. He gave me this tie.'

'Leith?'

'Yes. It's his old regiment. I can't remember which one. One day I ought to look it up in a book. He's very proud of it. Was.'

No one else arrived. A car appeared but it was merely to collect mourners from the previous ceremony, then they watched the cars turn, reverse, then move slowly through the gates, men staring ahead of them in profile, straight-backed, women eliminating their eyes, a child gazing out of a limousine with quiet pride. A man who appeared to be an official opened a door, glanced across towards the ante-room, then returned, closing the door and left Emily and Dowson alone, side by side, in a solitary vacuum, abandoned.

'Do you mind if I have one of your cigarettes?' Dowson asked.

'No, of course not.'

'Oh—no. You have only two left.'

'That's all right. Please take one.'

'Are you sure?'

'Yes.'

Dowson smiled and took a cigarette and lit it, then stood up and stared at a poster on the wall telling him that God Is All Merciful and that it was printed by Carthew & Sons of Bristol.

'What was the name of Virginia Woolf's husband?'

'Leonard,' Emily replied.

'That's right. Leonard. I remember reading his description of his wife's cremation after she had drowned herself. He said he asked the vicar, or whatever it was, for a particular piece of music by Beethoven to be played during the service. It had been a favourite piece of hers and he said they had noticed that it stopped at one point for a fraction of a second. A pause ... Then it continued. And that his wife had said it was the moment when the door should open and the coffin slipped away into the flames. During that beat. So he, Leonard, asked for it.'

Emily looked up at Dowson and then glanced away to avoid meeting his eyes as he continued:

'But they wouldn't play it. It was a small church and it was during the War and they didn't have the facilities, I suppose. They just played the usual requiem. Rather badly apparently. So that evening, Leonard Woolf listened to the piece of music himself in his home, sitting in his wife's chair, alone, next to the gramophone ... '

A pause, then:

'I wonder what Leith would have liked? I should have thought of it.'

But Emily didn't answer for she was already in tears.

A few minutes later the official reappeared and entered the ante-room and looked around, puzzled to see only two people there, and said:

'Mr Dowson? I'm sorry we're a bit late but we are rather running over schedule. But if you could come this way.'

They followed him across the yard into the opposite building and Emily stopped as she saw the empty pews and avoided looking further until she had sat down at the back, next to Dowson. The coffin was waiting before them within its grotesque shell, its edge against the left wall ready to be triggered efficiently into the flames of the crematorium at the simple press of a button. A small window of coloured glass, a token gesture of flowers in a stained vase, and a woman in a floral dress and felt hat sitting before a small church-organ studying the two of them as if she were window-shopping.

It was a short service, no more than eight minutes, and probably known in the trade as the basic minimum. A sermon that was as personal to the dead man as a monthly-magazine horoscope, followed by two verses of 'Jerusalem' (a standard fixture) which were sung only by the woman, since both Dowson and Emily merely stared at the metal cover of the coffin containing the body of Leith and thought of Korčula or Rome and the boat and the afternoon they had remained in bed while he lay in the gutter, and then of nothing whatsoever. Suddenly it was over. They heard the door slide open with a jolt, and a movement, a noise they couldn't detect, and then the door closed again till the next time.

'Goodbye, old sport,' Dowson said, quietly and without pretension. They then got up and walked out into the daylight and stood a few yards from each other as other cars arrived and other mourners were guided into the ante-room after the ashtrays had been emptied.

'Thank you,' Dowson said finally, turning towards Emily. 'For being here. I couldn't have sat through it otherwise.'

'But why was no one *else* here?' Emily asked, breaking once more into tears, the image of what was now happening to Leith suddenly splintering her mind.

'I don't know. I put announcements in the papers, both here and in California, but ... well, perhaps they were busy.'

Dowson gave a brief smile and then walked across to Emily and studied her, ignoring a chauffeur who was calling out to him to move out of the way.

'You look thinner. It doesn't suit you to be so thin. You know that.'

Emily made no reply and was suddenly aware that she was alone, after almost five months, face to face with Dowson, that he was standing by her, taking her hand and saying:

'Can I give you a lift? I've got a car waiting for me.'

Emily hesitated, trembling slightly, then asked:

'If ... if he hadn't died, like this, would we have seen each other again?'

'I don't know. But we have, and you haven't answered my question. Can I give you a lift home?'

'All right.'

Dowson looked at her then smiled. They then began to walk towards the gates, when the official was heard hurrying after them, polished shoes on gravel.

'Mr Dowson—may I ask, sir, what is your request concerning the ashes of the deceased?'

Dowson stopped and thought for a while, then took a piece of paper and wrote down an address and handed it to the official:

'Put the ashes in a box and send them to this man. He's a

film director who lives in Venice and I know how much the gesture would mean to him. Good day.'

*   *   *

When Emily returned to her flat, she was alone. It being the nanny's day off, I had acted the role of baby-sitter (or at least I had read a magazine and listened to the radio while Annabelle snoozed and the other children had been taken to a neighbour's tea party) and had heard a car arrive then leave almost immediately. In two minds whether to make tea or pour a whisky for Emily, since cremations are depressing affairs at the best of times, I decided on the whisky and was measuring two glasses when Emily entered, her face slightly flushed.

'Say nothing and drink this,' I said, handing her the glass.

'First I must tell you something.'

'After the whisky. Or if you prefer, after *my* whisky if you're going to tell me stories of weeping widows and sobbing fans.'

'No,' replied Emily, sitting on the edge of the armchair. 'Quite the contrary.'

And that really was that. Eight months later, Emily divorced Hallam and was granted custody of the children. On May 21st, 1969, she married Christopher Dowson in a Registry Office in Kensington, a ceremony that was attended by no more than four people including Martha Benenden and myself.

There were no photographs.

Part Three

DOWSON

Thirteen

It must be said immediately that if there is such a thing as a happy marriage, then the marriage between Emily and Dowson was, to the observer, happy. On the other hand, if you asked me to define the phrase 'happy marriage', I would change the subject, refer you to a book of aphorisms on the shelf behind you, or more likely pretend I was as deaf as Beethoven. I am neither brave enough nor arrogant enough to judge the relationship between a wife and a husband and I am not prepared to begin now, except to say that compared to other marriages I have witnessed, my first statement is as honest a generalization as I can offer. Emily told me she was happy and so indeed did Dowson and I see no reason to disbelieve them, though remember they have only been married a month. However the portents ought to be favourable.

After that pitiful wedding in Kensington in which they were bound till death by a man with a toupée, they went for their honeymoon to a village on the South Coast. They had resolved never to leave England, a country they both loved in their own way, more than any other, and they wanted to share their rediscovery now that it was summer once more and the blossom was fading. And so they drove to Dorset and rented a cottage on the cliffs and picnicked at night on the beach, lighting a bonfire on the sand.

During the months before the wedding, while solicitors bickered with each other, Emily fell deeper in love with Dowson as day followed day. He was always considerate, always patient when the strain of the divorce became unbearable and learnt to love the children (nervously at first as he struggled to be accepted as a father rather than as an uncle), each in their own individual way. And though Dowson rarely talked about his past ('Like yours, Emily, it is being cancelled out'), she learnt to understand him, not completely, for that was impossible, but more than anyone else. He had told her once, while they were making plans for the future, that he was a difficult man to live with and she had smiled in disbelief. It is superfluous to say that I saw less of Emily in the first few months — as indeed did everyone — but when I did, the happiness surrounding her was almost tangible, and she would ask me to lunch and tell me anecdotes about Dowson and the children, clutching my arm with pride, her eyes wide, beautiful. I envied her and Dowson together and hated myself for that. I didn't reveal that envy but it was there and I cannot deny it.

I would see it in the eyes of others, and more often I would hear it. They had just begun to forgive Hallam as they saw Emily in those months while Dowson was in Rome, saw her almost ready to be available once more. The men who had always loved her, and the ones who had just discovered her, suddenly had renewed hope, were prepared to make their bids at Sotheby's in order to acquire the possession that had belonged to someone else for so long. They had courted her and pursued her, waiting for the right moment, believing that in time, a mere season perhaps, she would consent and make her choice. She did and it was Dowson, appearing from nowhere, and once again they were brushed aside. The envy and the hatred returned, but a different hatred. Before, they had disliked Hallam simply because he was Emily's husband (Hallam, now, by the way, back in the fold) but they despised Dowson because he was just Dowson. They didn't understand him and they didn't care to try. On any terms, even if he had married a harpy, he would still have been their enemy. And so they skulked in doorways like conspirators in a Revenge Tragedy and waited. They had their ammunition, the gossip, the stories that had filtered back from the corners of Europe, and they waited. It may sound dramatic, even unreal, but that was how it was. I include myself in this, though mercifully only for a while, but it was there. Envy is a blind assassin and I have no defence.

*   *   *

After the honeymoon, Emily and Dowson lived in the house in Wiltshire, a small building set beside the Kennet, isolated in a village that had seen Regency carriages passing through from Marlborough and Chippenham. A simple garden, laid out by aunts and grandmothers to be discovered in stages (a bench in a corner beneath a willow, a lawn, another lawn, a fence dividing field, river, the languid profile of the hills beyond). An English garden with everything that that implies, to be enjoyed in idleness; where Emily could supervise the honeysuckle and the rhododendrons and worry about the greenfly, and where a book or the Sunday newspapers could be read in the shade of an elm. A garden, the house itself, painted white as a backdrop for the still-life of roses, and the rooms within. I myself have always admired the house, comfortable as a cushion, and it seemed exactly right in its Romantic aspect for Emily, and then, of course, for Dowson.

It is a home to explore, to discover books on shelves beneath the staircase, books that had been read by one generation then re-read by another, not in uniform collections but singly, set one beside the other with equal affection, novels, poems, welcome guests. An oval portrait on a wall by Raeburn, a small landscape, a drawing by Henry Lamb of his daughter Henrietta; a white porcelain figure of a young girl, naked and reading a book (*la derrière potelée*) on .the mantelpiece, a Pleyel piano with yesterday's music, a doll's house in a darkened corner. Bedrooms with sloping roofs, so that one stoops to see rectangles of trees and water and a barge passing by, and fading flowered wallpaper. Victorian childrens' annuals by one's bed, scrapbooks, screens, a framed sampler on one wall, a rural anachronism separated from the present age where only a telephone in the hall awaits to recognize the decade.

'*We never want to leave here,*' Emily wrote to me in June. '*We live like echoes of the past, undisturbed and tranquil. To describe our daily life would seem coy and pretentious, a chapter from George Eliot, to one who lives in London, but you must see it for yourself. There is no television, except in the children's nursery, no cinema nearby, so be prepared! We sit each evening and read and listen to music—Christopher has immersed himself in English music, so we eat, talk and wake to Elgar and Delius.*

We are dormice and this is our teapot and we dare anyone, except you, to lift the lid. But please visit and see us. Love,

Emily Dowson

I did accept the invitation in early July to stay for a weekend, sleeping in Mark and Thomas's room; they were still at school. Emily cooked lunch and we sat in the kitchen and I admired the curtains. I still found it difficult to talk to Dowson for he spoke hardly at all and seemed, though I may well be mistaken, totally remote. It was a strange sensation for this was not Stadshunt any more, but his own home, with his own wife, and yet he remained as elusive as he was at our first meeting. Perhaps it was shyness (that perennial explanation we utter to prove our sensitivity) or perhaps he simply had no interest in me whatsoever. Admittedly, I had not exactly welcomed the marriage with open arms but one must make allowances. I was prepared to be his friend for Emily's sake, was prepared to forget all the scandal I had heard and wanted to demonstrate that. Therefore, after lunch (in itself a delight, though pastry is not yet Emily's *forte*) I asked Dowson to show me around the village, and to my surprise, he agreed.

Leaving Emily with Annabelle, we crossed the bridge over the Kennet and made our way slowly towards the hills, (one boasting a horse of chalk), the sky cloudy although it was still warm.

'Are you lonely here?' I asked cautiously.

'No,' Dowson replied, then after a moment qualified this by saying: 'This is what I have always wanted. I was born in a city, lived in cities, lived among crowds as you do. But never this. The timelessness. This could be any age, almost any century, but it could only be England,' and he gestured back towards the village and the bridge, a cornfield beyond. 'Here I can observe … Notice things. Do you understand? The shape of a tree, the movement of a fish, the action of a moorhen, stand still for hours and observe the quiet sadness around us.'

'Sadness?' I asked, with surprise. 'Sadness perhaps that England everywhere else is changing, but you and Emily are anything but sad.'

'When I first saw her, she was sad. It was in a house I didn't know.'

'Stadshunt—'

'And she was sad, perhaps like England as you say. She was sad and that was when I fell in love with her.'

Dowson was quiet for a long while, then suddenly looked up at me and smiled:

'You were there, weren't you?'

'Yes.'

'As always … '

At the peak of the highest hill, three boys were flying a kite, a red-box affair that hovered over us. From this height we could see Marlborough and perhaps, on a clearer day, the towns beyond. We both sat on the grass and stared at the kite as it dipped and soared.

'I must admit,' I said, 'it was very courageous of you to take on four children.'

Dowson made no reaction, as if to imply that he never considered the situation a problem at all. There was a pause and then I said, not looking at him:

'By the way, did you ever go to Biarritz?'

A hesitation:

'Biarritz?'

'Yes.'

'Should I have done?'

'No ... It's just that someone thought they saw you there early last year.'

'Is that so? Look, they almost lost the kite. Did you see that?'

'So you've never been there?'

'Biarritz? No, I don't think so.'

'Must have been somebody else.'

There was a momentary silence, then we both got up to walk back down the hill, when Dowson said:

'Who said he saw me in Biarritz?'

'Oh, a friend of mine. Abel-Hardy. You don't know him.'

'But I do.'

'You do?'

'Of course. He was at Stadshunt. The day I saw Emily. I rather liked him.'

'Then he was mistaken?'

'Perhaps.'

When we returned to the house, Emily was in the garden, sitting on a bench, sewing a button on a child's blazer.

'You look exhausted,' she said, placing the needle neatly into the side of the cotton-reel. 'Christopher must have taken you to the top of Lady Hamilton.'

'Lady Hamilton?'

Emily laughed:

'Oh, that's our name for that highest hill. They're all named after notorious mistresses. At night when they're in silhouette, they all look like rows of enormous bosoms, except for one with a tree on top which rather spoils the imagery. Anyway, Lady Hamilton is the biggest and those on the end are Mrs Fitzherbert, and Lily Langtry is somewhere there, but I forget which. Christopher, which is Lily Langtry?'

But Dowson had gone. We called for him but he was neither in the house, the garden, nor the neighbouring field.

'He must have gone to the shops ... ' Emily said as we stood by the river and stared at the reeds, but by the expression in her voice I knew that she was attempting to convince herself that this was true. I suspected then, and later I learnt that I was right, that Dowson often disappeared without warning – as in Korčula and Rome – though at first only for a few hours or at most a day.

As it grew dark and he still hadn't returned Emily and I sat in the drawing-room and I asked her to play a favourite piece of music on the piano. She agreed but without enthusiasm, then stopped on the pretence that the Muse had deserted her and offered me a drink instead.

At night, in the country, in a house like this, the sounds are melancholy. A clock chiming in the hall, an owl, the rocking of a chair or even the sound of curtains being drawn. Both of us sat in deep cushioned armchairs opposite each other and I knew that Emily was listening for a footstep, for the door to open and for Dowson to appear. To distract her, I began to tell her absurd stories about friends in London, but I might as well as have been describing minor characters in an obscure novel, for they appeared to mean nothing to her. It was now ten o'clock and the fire had been lit as it suddenly grew cold.

'Emily ... I *am* happy for you. You know that.'

'Yes. Yes I do.'

'And your parents? Have they reconciled themselves to Christopher yet?'

'Oh, they will. You must admit it must have been a bit of a shock. Antony of course is non-committal, playing the officer role well, but Mummy still has the impression that Christopher is a plumber who seduced me on the *Brighton Belle* and only married me for my money.'

I smiled and asked tentatively:

'*Has* he any plans? I mean as far as working.'

'Oh, Christopher doesn't need to *work*—'

'I know, but has he any plans ... anyway?'

Emily glanced away, a slight tremor, then smiled and said: 'Of course he has!' and walked across to the drinks table and poured another sherry and stared out quickly through the curtains.

'Backgammon?' I suggested, changing the subject.

'No ... '

'Come on. You know you can always beat me if you try. When Christopher comes back he can play the winner. All right?'

Emily turned slowly and looked at me as I was unfolding the card-table.

'I love him,' she said.

I placed the table back against the wall and nodded:

'I know.'

'He's different from you and me. Different from anyone either of us have ever met or will. I know he's not easy to understand. But he's honest, and he's kind. In Korčula, I saw him with Leith and he was ... he was kind ... Unselfish. That's so rare ... '

She then turned away and sat down and stared into the fire.

'Does he never talk about his past?' I asked. 'I must admit

I'd be fascinated to know. He seems to have been everywhere.'

Emily suddenly smiled, then laughed:

'Oh, goodness yes. Simply everywhere. He gave me this which he bought in Rome. See?'

And she hurried to a shelf and showed me a beautifully bound copy of the poems of Petrarch.

'You see how kind he is. Oh, and I must show you these.'

Emily moved quickly, excitedly to a drawer and took out a small brooch, and then a *millefiore* paper-weight from a desk.

'Hold them in your hand. Aren't they marvellous?'

I agreed. They were exquisite and I asked her where he got them.

'Oh, that paperweight,' she replied, 'was from Florence. And the brooch he said was from France. I'm almost sure he said it was from Biarritz, but then of course I can't be certain.'

* * *

I was in bed when Dowson returned. I heard the front door close, then his footsteps on the stairs and then he entered the room next to mine. There was a silence, then I heard Emily moan, not in anguish but in that first enviable moment of inexplicable happiness.

The next morning I returned to London before anyone was awake, leaving a note of apology for not staying the full weekend, for I had forgotten completely about an unavoidable *thé dansant* that was being given by a maiden aunt.

149

Fourteen

He was called Christopher. It was not planned that way but he was introduced to the children as 'Christopher' and so it remained. Dowson himself had no objections since there seemed no alternative. He could hardly adopt a paternal name, since they were already attributed in varying degrees, from the more formal 'Papa' to the affectionate 'Daddy', to Hallam, and there was nothing he could do about it. And so it was Christopher, step-father to four children who accepted him without question, liked him without bribery and finally trusted him. He loved them and I believe they loved him, though they saw him rarely. Mercifully, Hallam himself assumed a role of apathy towards his children (he was already considering remarriage to a woman journalist from Bromley) and so the pressure was eased. Dowson talked little of this new role as step-father, but I know he didn't regret it, and certainly, even in my eyes, the children seemed to improve, seemed more relaxed and secure and were polite at tea-parties and said thank you for the sweets without being prompted.

In those summer months, when the school holidays began, the family would go on excursions throughout the county and beyond, visiting Longleat and Wilton and Stonehenge (big disappointment) or sailing on the Kennet and Avon Canal. The weather was kind, waking husband and wife each morning with sunlit panels of light on the sheets, allowing them to lie within each other's arms or to make love once more until the eldest child woke and knocked on the door and sat on the edge of the bed, shyly assessing the day. Then the other children would appear, clutching comics and submitting to their hair being brushed or being told to go back and wash their face again. They visited Avebury one day, driving in the car to the village and walking around the giant stones, taking photographs of each other for the album, and running into the dry ditch surrounding the ritual circle, then later had tea and cakes.

'I *am* nervous of them,' Dowson told Emily one night in bed. 'I want you to reassure me, want you to tell me that they have accepted me. I know I can never be their father. I know that one day one of them will accuse me or you, but I need them to love me because they are part of you. I hear Mark call me "Papa" by accident, as he did today without thinking, sitting in the car, and I am vulnerable. Grateful for that casual slip of the tongue, but vulnerable. I see their names on their exercise books, on school reports, and it is Hallam not Dowson and it always will be, at least for the boys. One side of me wants to smother them with presents and spoil them like puppies, while the other is in anguish whenever I correct them for even the slightest thing. I await one of them to turn on me and say "But you are not my father" if I administer the smallest discipline, but so far none of them have. I know you understand that and I ask not for sympathy but for reassurance. You must treat me as their father, then, in time, so will they.'

Emily had smiled and put her arms around him and said that, of course, she understood and that she didn't mean to be possessive and that it was simply the only security she had had when living with her first husband. Besides, she added, moving closer to him, moving her body on to his, kissing his neck, mouth, eyes, one day they could have a child of their own. A son perhaps who would be called Dowson and would always remain so.

'No.'

*   *   *

If I have given the impression that the Dowsons' marriage was one of total isolation, enforced by one or the other, then that it is not entirely true. Certainly they made no attempts to meet people, and it is natural for one to assume that this was because of Dowson himself, since Emily had always previously enjoyed the company of friends and acquaintances. Without doubt, Emily sensed a certain restlessness at times, both in herself and in her husband, and had once asked him, after he had been absent for almost half the night, where he had been. Dowson had not replied immediately, and then had said simply:

'It is changing. I want to observe it before it dies. They have already cut down two trees since spring from the river bank and soon there will be nothing ... I walk and observe. That is all.'

'Then may I come with you?'

'If you come with me, then I can't return to you,' Dowson had replied smiling and had kissed her gently and touched her hair framing her face, asking her never to cut it. To keep it in the same style as he had first seen her and Emily had agreed.

Nevertheless, apart from Dowson's brief journeys alone (which may have been merely the nocturnal rambles he said they were), the two of them *did* leave the house together, not only for the excursions as a family, but also to stay in Cumberland in the first week of July. The Bowness house was empty, three of the children had returned to school and Lady Bowness had suggested that Emily and Dowson (plus Annabelle) should spend a brief holiday there, alone and undisturbed. I cannot say if there was any reluctance on either part to accept the offer (it was, in fact, Dowson's first visit), but on July 3rd they drove north and arrived at the house by the lake, parking the car on the gravel in time for tea.

'Are you sure no one is here?' Dowson asked, gazing up at the front of the building and the rows of windows.

'I told you. Nobody's here — except of course Harwell and Anna.'

Dowson looked at her, startled:

'Deverell and Anna? Who on earth are they?'

'Well, Anna is my nanny,' Emily replied. 'Or was my nanny. And Deverell is her husband.'

'But you said *no one* was here.'

'None of the family, but Anna and Deverell are *always* here.'

'Then we're not alone.'

'But they won't take any notice. Besides, they live in the corner of the house. We'll never see them except at breakfast and things. Anna cooks, and Deverell — well, Deverell is the butler really.'

Emily smiled and turned towards Dowson as he stood at the boot of the car, not moving.

'What's the matter?' she asked, puzzled.

But Dowson didn't reply and took the suitcases and walked to the main door.

'Don't be angry with me,' Emily said, taking his arm. 'I just didn't want anybody here. Anybody at all. Don't you understand?'

'I'm sorry. I didn't think.'

There was a pause then Dowson nodded and smiled:

'Are you sure there's only the two of them? The house could contain a circus and two battalions. What about head gardener, gamekeeper and French maid?'

'Gardener perhaps,' Emily replied laughing, 'but I assure you, Mr Dowson, there is no French maid.'

'Quel dommage.'

As it happened, except for the initial introductions (*Do I call him Deverell or* Mister *Deverell?*) they were left alone. Emily's nanny was a Sunday-and-Holy-Day Catholic (her housemaid's knee encouraged by the church pew) and considered divorce with the same degree of vehemence as Thomas More, but instead of going to the Tower in protest, she went to the kitchen and remained there amid the copper pans, the silver cutlery and, of course, the chopping block. It was a dramatic gesture that Emily regretted and Dowson ignored —except to taste the food with caution. He liked Deverell however, though he could never adjust himself to the idea of servants, and on the first day went out of his way to treat the butler as an equal until he realized that this embarrassed the man and so in turn embarrassed Dowson. It made him aware of the immense difference between his background and Emily's and though that might not be the sole reason for avoiding her society of friends, it was undoubtedly part of it.

'It makes me uneasy,' Dowson told Emily during their first dinner at the house, 'to see a man twice my age bow and call me *Sir*. It makes me uneasy not only because I see him play the servant but because he expects *me* to play the master. And I can't. It's not a question of protocol or upbringing but of attitude.'

'It doesn't show,' Emily said, as if in encouragement.

'But it's a role,' he replied. 'It's another part for me to play ... '

Dowson then hesitated and stared, not at his wife, but at the candelabra, the silver pheasant, a portrait of someone who had died at Ramillies.

'Emily ... I wish I could reveal my feelings more easily. Express them. But ... I keep them in darkness like that poor woman in the kitchen who needs a cupboard in a church and a grille dividing her from the world in order to bare her soul.'

'But why are you saying this? Just because Deverell —'

'Not just because of him. But because ... '

A pause, Dowson blushed slightly then was silent and concentrated on the trout that had been caught that morning. Across the table, Emily looked at him, then glanced away before his eyes met hers. It seemed as if her husband was trying to communicate to her but had failed and she felt helpless. She thought of a question she could ask, something that might bring her closer to him but it was too late. Deverell had entered the room to refill the wine glasses, was asking if coffee was required, and the moment was gone. As in Rome with Leith, the mask had returned, not only to Emily's regret but also, it is certain, to Dowson's as well. In everything that I know about him (and I am cautious to offer an opinion) I believe that Dowson wanted to be understood, wanted to be accepted for what he was but feared rejection. Consequently, over the years he had become evasive, had escaped from himself and was aware of it. If I am right I don't know the cause, nor perhaps will I ever, but then in the age of Freud we are all Freudians and to hell with it. Let's stick to the facts. They may not speak for themselves, but they're infinitely more reliable than parlour diagnoses. Thus: after the trout, lemon sorbet, followed by coffee (Blue Mountain), brandy, bed and pranks.

The next day, Emily took Dowson for a walk around the estate. They had already spent an hour touring the house, visiting the nursery, her childhood bedroom, the library, the attics, Grumble's kennel, and had decided, on this warm day in July, to stroll along the lake and into the woods and fields that surrounded it. Annabelle was left with Anna (tearful submission on both parts) and then husband and wife walked hand in hand, not hurrying but taking their time, alone and secure. They talked — at least Emily talked and Dowson listened — then crossed from pebbles on to grass moving uphill until they reached a stream set deep in a gulley of silent pines. There they made love like mischievous children, giggling, holding their breath as something passed near them (a cow, Guernsey), Emily moving her bottom to avoid one pine-cone only to find another, then Dowson running down the bank into the stream and shouting as he discovered that the water was as cold as ice. Emily felt idyllic and excited, enjoying being the scandalous daughter of the lord of the manor (*ah, les romans de ma jeunesse*) and wanting secretly to be discovered as she lay naked in the grass under the sun. The Talk Of The Village. If Only Mama Could See Me Now.

'She'd string me up from one of her precious acacias,' Dowson said, lying next to her, 'and make me tug my forelock like the peasant I am.'

'Tug your what?'

'Forelock.'

'Oh – I thought you said something else.'

'Mrs Dowson, as a daughter of the aristocracy, you really have the filthiest mind.'

'But don't you know – we upper class women always have had. We pick our noses and dream of passionate rape with the stable boy.'

Dowson laughed and kissed her shoulder and neck:

'And to think,' he said, 'that I married such a degenerate creature.'

'You almost didn't.'

A sudden pause, then Dowson lifted his head and looked at her and saw a sudden trace of sadness in her eyes, then she turned away, obscuring her face with her hair.

'Are you talking about Korčula?' he asked quietly.

No answer.

'Emily, if you're talking about Korčula, all I can say is that I was frightened of asking you to marry me, even to stay another day, in case you refused. That's why I left. Then when I saw you in London and you hadn't changed –'

Emily stared up at him quickly:

'Why should I have changed? Do you mean my feelings towards you?'

'No, not only that ... '

156

'What then?'

Dowson didn't reply for a moment:

'Nothing,' he said finally. 'We'd better get dressed.'

He stood up and moved towards his clothes.

'But what else might have changed?' Emily insisted.

Dowson kept his back to her as he dressed, then turned, folded his arms and studied her, head on an angle as if she were the prize exhibit in a raffle:

'You know, Mrs Dowson, you really have the most delightful bottom I have ever seen. If Chippendale were here now, he'd design his chairs for you.'

Emily's clothes were then thrown to her and Dowson began to walk away, not even looking back when he heard Emily shout 'Why don't you answer my question?' but kept moving steadily downhill as Emily, swearing under her breath, struggled into her clothes (pants, dress, the basic layers), ran after him, ran back for her shoes, then followed him six paces behind in silence.

After twenty minutes, the house came into view again, and the driveway and then they both stopped as they saw the Land-Rover, its doors open, Grumble sniffing around the wheels.

'Oh no,' Emily said, pulling a face.

'Who is it?'

'I'm not sure, but I think it's Henry Waterford. He's a friend of Antony.'

'But Antony's not here.'

'No. But I am.'

*   *   *

They didn't stay. Waterford was pleasant enough (though he called Dowson 'Edward' twice) but they didn't stay, even for another night. They packed their suitcases, placed a blanket in the back seat of the car for Annabelle to sleep and drove back that evening for Wiltshire. Emily apologized to Deverell and his wife for the sudden decision to leave, said that she would write, but the departure, for her, was regretted.

'We could have waited till after dinner, at least,' Emily said to Dowson as the car moved through the darkness. 'Anna had made a casserole especially. She tried to hide it but it was gesture of peace towards us.'

There was no reply and Emily stared at the headlights on the road ahead, the ribbon of cat's-eyes unfolding before them, a road-sign looming up and passing them by.

'What did it say?' Dowson asked.

'What?'

'The sign.'

'I have no idea.'

'You're supposed to be navigating.'

'I know the road.'

'That's what you said on the way up and we almost ended up in a field.'

'That wasn't my fault —'

'Don't shout. You'll wake up Annabelle.'

'I'm *not* — I'm not shouting,' Emily replied, her voice dropping to a whisper. 'Anyway ... once we get to Kendal, it's straight down on the M6.'

'I hate motorways.'

'It's the quickest way.'

'I know.'

Silence. Within an hour, they were moving fast and by-passing Lancaster. At this speed they could be home by dawn. For a while Emily dozed off, waking up momentarily as the car slowed down through a town or stopped for petrol, attempting to take stock of where they were and then falling asleep again. When she finally awoke completely, the light was already appearing in the sky and they were on a smaller, emptier road crossing open fields. She glanced back to see that Annabelle was still asleep (mouth open, blanket on the floor) then looked at Dowson. At first she thought he was unaware of her gaze until he said, remaining in profile:

'Sleep well?'

'Had a dream about Leith.'

'Good or bad?'

'Can't remember really. He was in England.'

'Then it was good,' Dowson said and held out his hand towards her. 'Friends?'

Emily smiled and took it:

'Yes.'

'We'll be going through Cheltenham in a few minutes. Another hour at the most and we'll be home.'

Dowson then lit a cigarette and studied the approaching lights of the town. Unlike Emily, though he drove well, he was reluctant to drive over-fast. Seventy miles an hour was his limit, except when he was on his own.

'I was thinking ... ' he said. 'About Edward. Edward Hallam. And that hearty Henry we just met.'

'He was harmless.'

'I envy them. Edward and him. Deverell. All of them.'

'What on earth for?' Emily asked, surprised.

'Because they knew you before I did. Knew you when you were younger.'

'I was fat and spotty with big teeth.'

'But Edward knew you for ten years. Since you were sixteen. His marriage was very lucky.'

'Not for me, Christopher. *This* marriage is lucky. Not because we grew up together, but because we'll be able to grow old together.'

Dowson suddenly looked at her, startled, taking his eyes off the road, staring at her with almost a look of panic until Emily shouted a warning (corner, tree, wall) and there was a sliding, a locking of brakes as Dowson pulled the wheel round, bouncing the car in its skid off the wall itself then bringing it to a discreet halt on the kerb, headlights illuminating a shop window.

'Are you all right?' Emily asked anxiously.

Dowson switched off the engine and glanced at one or two people who were approaching, disappointed to find that the accident was merely trivial. In the back seat, Annabelle turned over in her sleep and made herself more comfortable.

'Yes. I'm all right.'

*   *   *

On July 23rd, Emily would be twenty-nine years old. In celebration, two of her friends, Michael and Virginia, who owned a large house near Salisbury, invited her and Dowson to a weekend party. It was refused. The letter was taken out of its envelope by Emily then mentioned casually in a dismissive way, as if it really didn't matter.

'They're just friends who've been kind to me, but I know they'll understand if we say no … '

Dowson didn't answer and so the subject was dropped and the letter thrown away.

That same afternoon, however, there was a telephone call (a rare occurrence in the past months as friends learnt to expect the refusals when they sent invitations) and Emily answered it. It was from Virginia.

'Just to confirm, Emily, when you're arriving. We can pick you up at the station if you want to come by train.'

'Well … I'm not sure —' Emily began.

'Then come by car. It's only half an hour. You've got to come, both of you. Do you realize we haven't seen you for absolutely months. No one has.'

Emily was about to reply when her husband entered, closing the door, and stood in the hallway looking at her. She hesitated, almost guilty:

'No. I'm sorry,' she said into the phone and quickly put down the receiver.

'Virginia is very insistent,' she said, turning away, a slight blush on her face.

'So it seems,' and then: 'Did you want to go?'

'No, of course not. It was just silly of me to mention it before. This is where I want to be. Here, in this house with you. Nothing else.'

And Emily took his arm and held him close and they walked out into the garden to see if any of the roses needed pruning. Later, they went to bed and made love until it was time for the children's tea. These were her happiest moments, lying in bed with Dowson, holding him close, seeing him beside her, touching him, merely knowing that he was there. Sometimes they would talk about the children, or about the house, and the land surrounding it, but mostly they were silent and Dowson would repeat that he loved her. That afternoon as they heard the children playing outside (Victoria inheriting her grandmother's voice. That perpetual decibel), Dowson suddenly said:

'The yellow dress. You don't wear it any more.'

'Which yellow dress? Heavens, Mark's fallen over again.'

'The yellow dress you wore in Korčula. You don't wear it any more.'

'*That* one? Oh, Christopher, it's over two years old. Styles have changed since then. One day Mark's going to fall in the river. We ought to repair that fence.'

'I'd like you to wear it.'

'But it's far too short. Anyway —'

'And the blue one. With the flowers. The fuchsias. You never wear that either.'

'Oh, don't be silly. They're much too out of fashion. I can't possibly wear them now.'

Dowson looked at her, moved away and looked at her for a long time, then without saying another word he got dressed and left the room. Emily didn't move, staring at the door, hearing his footsteps on the stairs, then she walked to the wardrobe and took out the yellow dress from behind the rows of others and looked at it, placing it against her body as she stood before the mirror. It *was* too short and it needed ironing but perhaps she could wear it after all. Just around the house or to the shops.

At five-twenty, the telephone rang again. I state the time because it was myself who phoned. Virginia had asked me to persuade Emily to stay the weekend, saying that they had a surprise for her, it being her birthday, and that she simply couldn't remain hidden away like a nun for ever. 'It's just not like her,' Virginia had said. 'Emily of all people.' I agreed that it certainly was not like the Emily we used to know but I assured Virginia that she and Dowson were happy and preferred to be alone. When they decided to meet other people they would, but until then there was nothing anyone could do. 'But you could *try*,' Virginia had insisted. 'We all know that *he's* the one who's keeping her there. It's bloody selfish. He's behaving like some Victorian squire.' Hardly a squire, I replied, but I promised I would try. And so I did and Dowson answered the telephone.

'Christopher?' I began. 'I'm glad you answered the phone. Emily can't hear, can she?'

'No.'

'Well, it's just that Michael and Virginia know that next Tuesday is Emily's birthday and they've planned this surprise which even I don't know about. A celebration surprise, so you've just got to try and persuade her to come, won't you?'

There was a silence at the other end of the telephone and for a moment I thought we had been cut off (*le vice anglais*), or worse, that Dowson would just put the receiver down. But finally he answered:

'How many people are going to be there?'

'At Michael's? Oh, I don't know. No more than a dozen at the most. You'd like Michael, and the atmosphere is very relaxed. Besides, it's all a special treat for Emily. For her birthday.'

There was another silence and I was convinced that I had succeeded, when suddenly Dowson asked me a question that startled me.

'How old would she be?'

'Who?'

'Emily. On her birthday.'

My first reaction was to laugh, passing the question off as a joke, but it was repeated. Dowson simply didn't know.

'Twenty-nine,' I said.

'Twenty-nine ... ' he echoed, almost with a trace of regret, though I couldn't be sure.

'Then you'll come?'

'I'll talk to her,' replied Dowson and put the phone down. What on earth, I thought, does one make of that?

*   *   *

The next morning, it being sunny, Dowson suggested to Emily that they ought to take a boat along the Kennet, just the two of them. They would leave the children with the housekeeper who lived across the other side of the green, and take a boat along the river, with a hamper and wine, or perhaps stop at a pub somewhere near Devizes. Emily had agreed immediately and so it was arranged. As she told me long after, it was one of the happiest days of her marriage so far and also the day she began to understand much more about the man she had met in Korčula and then married. I can't say I fully agree with her for the enigma remains but then I myself wasn't there.

They decided to take the boat westwards, drifting idly

between willows and under bridges, past Wilcot and All Cannings, moving languidly over the water, Emily lying on cushions at the rudder, her face shaded by a straw hat, Dowson at the oars, white trousers and blue shirt, opposite her.

'You appear to be dreaming,' he said, smiling. 'Daydreaming. I should tell you a story like Lewis Carroll. This is not the Isis and you're not Alice, thank God, but the mood is here.'

'Lewis Carroll, if you recall, only told stories to little girls, not mothers of four children.'

'But I repeat, the sentiment is here.'

'Towards little girls perhaps,' smiled Emily, one hand in the water.

'But I *like* little girls. Preferably about eleven years old. Blonde hair, hands folded in lap, eyes lowered.'

Emily looked up at him:

'I do hope, Mr Dowson, you don't have a little girl in mind. I might be jealous.'

'But I have. Her name is Victoria.'

And Dowson laughed, encouraging Emily, and she moved forward and kissed him so that the boat almost became stranded in the reeds.

'We're very lucky, aren't we?'

Emily nodded:

'Yes. Very ... '

'If only we could be like that church in the village.'

'You mean grey and draughty with a point sticking out of our head?'

Dowson smiled and said:

'It's been there seven hundred years and hasn't changed. It's seen Welsh kings and Scots kings and German kings, weddings and funerals. Births. And nothing has changed it. The men who built it died before the Crusades and it's still there. Unchanged ... Lucky church.'

'Lucky us,' replied Emily.

'I spent half the night once in that church.'

'Ooh—too many ghosts.'

'Yes. Too many.'

Idleness, drifting (a barge passing by, someone in green polishing a square of brass), until they reached a pub on the banks of the Kennet; small, named after one of the king's arms, with an apron of lawn set out with tables above the water. A waitress created by Dickens, or waiting to be.

The two of them, husband and wife, sat outside on the grass, a table isolated from the rest, and ordered salad and beer, sitting beneath a large elm-tree, the rowing-boat moored beneath them, scattered cushions, the oars side by side.

'I'm sure this hasn't changed either,' Emily said casually.

'What?'

'The view. Like the church, it hasn't changed. The same hills, river—'

'Oh, but it has,' Dowson interrupted. 'Not dramatically, but it has changed. Trees have been cut down or died. Others have been planted. The river itself has widened or narrowed its banks. It has changed because it is living. As we are. It is only when something is dead that it doesn't change. Physically, of course, it changes, but not the memory. The image of the person remains as we ourselves choose it. And if someone we love dies young, unseen, then she is always young.'

'Like your mother?'

Dowson didn't reply—across the river, a game of cricket. The sound of the ball out of synchronization when struck by the bat—then he said:

'Leith told me once that people always expected him to look like he was in *Robin Hood*, even though he made the film thirty years ago. That was their image of him and they were disappointed when they saw an old man. They resented him for that as if it were his fault that he had changed. But those who never saw him, never met him, would always picture Leith as the athletic young hero they first saw in the cinema. They wanted him to remain like that and so he did in their minds. That is why I have never returned to the village in Yorkshire where I lived as a child, because as long as I don't see it, my memory of it, false and over-romantic as it may be, will always be the same ... '

He hesitated, glanced at Emily, then signalled to the waitress for some more drinks.

Much of what was said that day, Emily wrote down in her diary. There are merely notes, questions to herself, resolutions. On one page she had written: *He told me that he had loved four people in his life, and that three of them were dead. I assume his mother was the first, and Leith perhaps another, but I don't know who the third person was. I suspect it was a girl he had had an affair with. In fact I am sure of it. A girl who had died. How or why I don't know. I asked but he said he would tell me another day.* Undoubtedly, this was Celia Batleigh. I have not told Emily this fact for she will, I assume, learn it for herself.

On another page, she elaborates Dowson's obsession (for so it appears to me) with the illusion of memory, the permanence of youthful death. *The timelessness and sadness*, as he told me on that first walk through the village, and in a way I accept his philosophy on the superficial level. One can argue whether Keats or Alexander the Great would be revered as much if they had died deaf and dribbling in a geriatric ward, or if Christ himself had ended his days bald and toothless, dying of influenza at the age of ninety. But these are mere after-dinner assumptions, and I myself cannot take Dowson's theories too seriously. However, there is still the question why he chose finally to return to live in England, after twelve years as a wanderer, for the answer must be connected with his choice of Emily, first as a lover, then as a wife. In short, I fear the answer is sinister, as if Emily represented this picture-book England which he sought. To me, the cynic, I consider it lyrical and idyllic only to the dreamer, but to the realist, his idea of England is as dead as a dodo and almost as useless. But then there could be a hundred permutations and it is too easy (and dangerous) to interpret them from afar. Events may bear me out or may prove my thesis ridiculous, but that finally is for you to decide. Let us forget, therefore, that I used the word 'sinister'.

On the return journey back to the house, it seemed that rain would at last enter the English summer. Clouds appeared and modestly covered Lady Hamilton's bosom, and a breeze began to disturb the reeds, sending animals and moorhens into hiding. Dowson appeared to have forgotten the conversation at lunch, as if it never existed, and was in good spirits.

They tied the boat just near the bridge and Emily said she would go and collect the children from Mrs Powell. She began to move towards the green (already Victoria was running towards her, an embroidery frame in her hand, the similarity in her appearance to her mother uncanny) when Dowson called his wife's name. Emily turned and waited for him to say something but he merely looked at her, studying her carefully, as if for the first and last time, his eyes covering every inch of her body from hair to feet until she began to feel self-conscious.

'*You* must never change,' said Dowson quietly. 'Never.'

Emily smiled nervously and replied:

'I am not a church. You see, I have already changed in the eighteen months since we met. I have grown older and next week I am twenty-nine.'

'I know,' he said. 'And we are going to celebrate the fact. Not the age, but the birthday.'

'How?' Emily asked.

'With your friends. Michael and whoever he's married to. For the weekend.'

'Virginia ... '

'You'd like to go, wouldn't you?'

Emily hesitated then nodded. Dowson then smiled and walked through the side-gate of the house, his arm around Victoria's shoulders, asking her what special game they could play now.

The isolation, for better or worse, appeared to be over.

Fifteen

The lines were no more than half an inch in length, parallel to each other, the base of each one almost meeting but not quite. There was a bridge of a third line if the eyebrows were contracted, then a series of smaller lines, like gradient symbols on a map, unnoticed before and fanning out on the plain of the forehead itself. Then at the corners of the eyes, other shadows, creases, darts, seemed to have appeared no more than minuscule arrows under the harsh light, but they were there and they always would be.

The skin itself seemed to have revealed its pores almost overnight, and the more that Emily studied them in the mirror, the more they took on grotesque dimensions, a pitted lunar landscape on her cheeks, forehead and chin. Of course, they could be attributed to the sun or over-tiredness or the unflattering light, but they were undeniable. Each expression produced its own contribution to the basic features of her face, overlapping, dissolving, a minor furrow beneath lower lip, the mouth suddenly in the parentheses of arcs from nose to jaw, viciously described as *laugh lines* by a forgotten sadist. Then the neck itself, the shoulders, deeper shadows beneath the breasts. The more she observed the more she saw, until it seemed that not one square centimetre remained without its mocking gesture to her fading youth. She saw Age before her, the beginning of that gradual corrosion that all the creams, oils and foundations in the world could not impede. It was there in the mirror before her, staring at her defiantly. She was approaching her thirtieth year and nothing now could disguise that. She was getting old and it terrified her.

'What on earth are you standing pulling faces there for?'

Emily spun round, startled, moving quickly away from the light and saw Dowson at the door of the bedroom holding Victoria's hand.

'Oh, nothing,' Emily replied quickly, turning her back on them, one hand reaching for some cleansing cream.

'Well, just to tell you,' Dowson said, 'that Victoria and I have invented a new game.'

'It's a special-special game,' Victoria added, smiling. She was wearing a white dress and her blonde hair loose, looking her prettiest now that she was eleven years old. She had gone through a stage of plainness and overweight, but in the past summer seemed to have developed in grace and confidence, partly due to the fact that she had acquired by imitation many of the mannerisms and much of the elegance of her mother. 'Christopher and I always invent special-special games, like the treasure hunt.'

Emily didn't reply, smoothing the cream into her forehead, fingers moving from the centre to the temple, as she sat before the more flattering dressing-table mirror.

'It's all to do with the initial letters of flowers,' Dowson explained, moving across the room so that he could see her reflection. 'One of us chooses a flower, like "geranium" say, and the other has to find flowers in the garden whose initials make up the word *geranium*. That's a difficult one but it helps Victoria remember the names of flowers.'

'Hyacinth is worst,' said Victoria. 'Because of the y.'

'Why don't you join us?' Dowson asked.

'Later,' replied Emily. 'I've got things to do first.'

She saw Dowson studying her, then he nodded and looked at Victoria:

'Come on then. You can begin.'

And they left, closing the door. Emily heard Victoria suddenly laugh on the stairs, then another door was slammed shut and she heard them outside. For a long while, Emily didn't move, then finally walked to the window, one half of her face moist with the cream, and stared down at the garden. Victoria was standing on the lawn in her attitude of concentration (head on an angle, lower lip under upper teeth, left eye screwed up, gazing into space) while Dowson stood a few feet away, arms folded, smiling and waiting patiently, his full concentration on the young girl's face.

Emily moved away, drawing the curtains against the light, turning the room and her appearance into a gauze of soft shadow.

*　　*　　*

DEAR VIRGINIA　IMPOSSIBLE TO COME FOR WEEKEND　MANY REGRETS AT SUCH SHORT NOTICE BUT AM IN BED WITH FLU APOLOGIES APOLOGIES TO MICHAEL WILL PHONE

LOVE EMILY

*　　*　　*

On August 15th, Dowson was away from the house from dawn till mid-afternoon. This was not unusual and Emily was not unduly worried, for her husband had never been absent for more than a few hours, and certainly never more than a day. She knew that he enjoyed being alone, walking, or sometimes but rarely taking the car, and it gave her an opportunity to make herself as beautiful as she could. Furthermore, she remembered her life with Hallam when he had been in the house all day (under the guise of writing a screenplay that was talked about and never written) and the strain of constantly being within each other's sight had reached screaming pitch. That, more than his affairs, had eventually led to the breakdown of the first marriage and she was relieved that it was not being repeated in the second. She no longer sought explanations from Dowson, accepting that he was different from other people, aware of her lack of experience of men, and believed that he was simply exorcizing the restlessness that had plagued him since he was a child. This particular day, however, was not like the others. For when she went downstairs to breakfast, she discovered that he had taken Victoria with him as well.

'But didn't you see her leave?' Emily asked Annabelle, vainly trying to attract the child's attention across the table.

Annabelle, who shared the same room, merely shook her head and asked if she could get down.

'But you must have *heard* something?'

'I heard the car,' said Thomas casually. 'It wouldn't start at first. It kept making a lot of noise and woke me up.'

Emily hurried to the garage and the car was gone, and she stood in the road, staring up towards the green and the swings, then back in the direction of the bridge. There was no one to be seen except two boys leaning over the river-wall, bicycles propped beside them, bottle and straw fixed between the handlebars.

At three-thirty, she saw the car (a Morris) return and watched from the drawing-room window as Victoria, her face flushed and grinning, a straw hat on her head, got out and opened the rear door and took out two large baskets. Dowson appeared and the first glimpse of him was in profile as he emerged round the back of the car. He was wearing a white suit and a pale yellow shirt and was taking one of the baskets from his step-daughter. *It is Mrs Hallam, isn't it?*

Emily waited for them to discover her, sitting elegantly in a chair with the light behind her, wearing a long silk dress, as if posing for a portrait by Gerard or Ingres. The image was shattered, however, as Victoria entered noisily and thrust a purple-stained basket on to her lap.

'Look, Mama, see what we've got? Blackberries. Christopher and I must have collected *pounds*!'

Dowson arrived with the other basket and smiled and kissed Emily gently on the cheek.

'Victoria has the energy of a steam-engine. I am afraid I'm only responsible for a quarter of all this. A white suit is not ideal wear for blackberries.'

And Dowson grinned and added: 'You look very beautiful,' then touched her hair. Emily blushed slightly and looked at the blackberries, then at Victoria, who was beaming proudly, hands behind her back, her lips stained.

'You can make jam.'

'Or pies,' Emily said.

'Jam *and* pies. There's pounds. Christopher said it would be a surprise.'

'It is. It is a surprise.'

Victoria giggled then glanced up at Dowson then hurried to the door:

'I'm going to tell the others.'

'Where else did you go?' Emily called after her. 'What about lunch?'

'Oh, we had that at a pub. They let us into the garden, just on the river. Then we visited Stourhead and saw Alfred's Tower and the temples, and we saw the horrible motorway they're building and oh, lots of things. Bye.'

The door was slammed shut.

'She obviously enjoyed herself,' Emily commented quietly, placing the baskets on a table.

'Yes,' replied Dowson and lit a cigarette and studied the garden through the window.

'I've never been to Stourhead,' Emily said, not looking at him. 'Perhaps we could go together one day. Before the summer's over.'

Dowson didn't answer. Instead he opened the doors that led out on to the lawns, stopping only to say:

'The dress you're wearing. It's the same one you wore when I first saw you at Stadshunt.'

'Is it?' Emily replied quickly. 'I never noticed ... '

'Yes, I believe it is. It's only because you're wearing it during the day. Otherwise I would not have recognized it.'

'But you still like it?'

Dowson looked at it, then shrugged impartially and walked away to see if the grass needed cutting.

That evening, when the children were in bed, Dowson took out Emily's photograph albums that documented her life since she was a child. Large folios with flowered covers and grey pages, the pictures and clippings gummed in, many cut out of magazines and newspapers, when she was constantly being photographed by fashionable photographers at fashionable occasions.

Emily watched from the armchair as her husband turned over each page, silently, studying her face in all its infinite attitudes against a myriad backgrounds.

'Is this you at eight or is it Victoria?'

Emily stood up and gazed at the face of a young girl in half-profile, sitting on a pony.

'Me. The pony was called Kitchener.'

Other pages were turned over, other volumes opened. Puberty, the first dance, Emily and a girl called Candida at Tintagel, flash-bleached faces of girls with young men in bow-ties and crinkly hair, Antony in uniform, a dog (Grumble), the wedding day with Hallam ('Don't look at those'), Emily in the maternity bed ('Those teeth. Weren't they awful?'), Emily with her children in oilskin waterproofs. Emily on Loch Fyne with James, at yet another wedding (Tristram's), in a bikini on Corfu, in a London garden with a group of friends from Notting Hill Gate, posing in absurd positions with hats on their heads.

'That's Bindel, who's the poet you met,' Emily said,

pointing to a man in the photograph wearing a stetson, 'though it was taken four years ago. And that's Martha of course. Me. Derek who's a painter. I don't know who that is. He's a sculptor. Kenneth. Candida again. Oh, and that beautiful girl there is someone called Celia Batleigh. She died about six months after this. We all went to her funeral. It was very sad. You can't tell what she looked like there, but she was marvellous. You would have adored her.'

*   *   *

Two days later, on the 17th, Dowson took Victoria out again. They walked to the top of one of Lily Langtry's breasts and planted a paper Union Jack on the approximate position of her nipple, then walked back down again in time for lunch.

That night, as he had not done for the past week, Dowson did not make love to Emily. A quarrel ensued, suddenly, without warning and yet with relief, a storm after the cloying pressure of a heatwave. In the shouting and screaming, both husband and wife hurt each other verbally (an ashtray was thrown but it hit the wall) as deeply as they could. And then they stopped. Dowson opened the door and went downstairs and remained in the drawing-room throughout the night, not sleeping, sitting in the armchair next to the piano and the photograph album, looking at the pictures once again for a while, then just waiting to watch the dawn. Upstairs Emily, as always, wrote in her diary.

It is difficult to understand the emotional state of a woman at the best of times, but at Emily's age there appears a sudden and profound feeling of insecurity, often exaggerated but acute nevertheless. It can be seen in many external actions of women around thirty; jealousy of younger or prettier girls, a withdrawal from social gatherings where she might feel old, a desire to wear clothes that are either too young or too old, a passion to accomplish some worthy task of self-respect and the stubborn fear of beginning it. It manifests itself in excuses, a minor paranoia that every action she makes is being judged whether it be as simple as washing a cup. She seeks older friends and sycophants, prefers to be forty years old, visits doctors and psycho-therapists, resents her children growing older and her husband's success, indulges in the absurdities of flirtations, drugs, drink and all the other melodramatic symptoms of her age. These, of course, are generalizations, Digest observations, but I have seen them many times, especially in London.

As far as Emily is concerned, however, I am impressed. She did not attempt an escape; she merely remained as she was, in her house, as always, and wrote down, as at this moment, what she felt. It is simple and direct: she is fright-ened of being almost thirty and cannot explain why. That is all. She needs attention and flattery and sympathy but will not seek it. That is all. I haven't read the pages, but Emily described the gist of them to me, and I, for one, don't believe a single word of it. If what she has written is what I suspect, then it might as well be gibberish and Emily knows it. So, indeed, does Dowson.

Before the children awoke that morning, he returned to the bedroom and walked slowly to the desk where Emily was writing. She immediately covered the pages with her hand but Dowson made no effort to read them. He merely took his shirt from the back of the chair and began to dress, ignoring her. When he had finished, he said:

'Your best friend is Martha Benenden, isn't she?'

Emily hesitated, puzzled.

'According to the albums, you've known her since you were twelve and she appears to be your best friend. Am I right?'

'Well, yes ... I suppose she is,' Emily replied.

'Then why don't you go and see her?'

Emily looked at Dowson as he put on his shoes, trying to think of something to say, but thinking of nothing whatsoever. She looked at the pages before her, then finally said:

'If you want me to.'

'Go back to bed and get some sleep,' Dowson replied. 'I'll get the children's breakfast.'

He then left the room and there was silence, then she heard a piece of music by Elgar being played on the record-player in the drawing-room.

The next day, she telephoned Martha, and on the Thursday took the car and drove alone to Stadshunt.

*   *   *

In many ways, Emily's visit to the Benendens was similar to the time she went there over a year before when Dowson was in Italy. There was the same nervousness, the same desire on Emily's part to talk and yet when the opportunity arose (she and Martha sitting in a kitchen garden that was as precise and ordered as a knitting pattern) Emily found there was nothing she could say. She attempted to phrase sentences in her mind, but her fears about her husband suddenly appeared trivial, for in truth, he had done nothing to threaten the marriage or her happiness in any way. It was all in her imagination, coupled with the absurd bouts of depression that she knew were probably only temporary. So instead, she found herself listening to Martha, listening to her problems, pleased that she herself had decided to remain silent. Other people's marital difficulties often appear so ludicrously simple to solve and that is a great comfort. 'Honestly, Emily, I really believe he loves his horses more than me and that's the most frustrating thing. I can scratch another woman's eyes out, but what can I do about something with four legs and a tail that wins races at Newmarket?

All I can do is dream that it breaks a leg so that I can load the pistol and hand it to Rupert.'

They decided to eat in a hotel restaurant in Warwick, since Martha had to buy weekend supplies and Emily had planned to buy herself some new clothes. And so they drove there (a journey of no more than twenty minutes), taking the road than ran across Edgehill, with Martha at the wheel of her car, obeying the speed limit to the inch.

'By the way,' she said suddenly, 'hope you don't mind Rupert joining us for lunch with a friend of his?'

'As long as it's not a horse,' replied Emily.

'Not this time. Actually, he's rather nice, though pompous and boozy. I'm sure you don't know him.'

'What's his name?'

'*Stupid* bloody driver! What? Oh, Charles Pettison. He used to go out with Lucy Blakewell after she left Bridges.'

'No. Never met him.'

'Well, he's fat and insipid like all Lucy's boy friends, so you needn't worry about Christopher being jealous.'

'I don't think Christopher's the jealous type.'

'Isn't he? Well, if *I* was a man married to you I'd be as jealous as hell.'

Emily smiled and was silent and stared out at the hedges until they reached Warwick.

Pettison was in fact exactly as Martha had described him (wispy hair, red face, champagne paunch) and was waiting drunkenly with Rupert in the beamed and flock-papered bar of the hotel.

'You wouldn't believe it,' Martha whispered as they approached the men, 'but he used to be very attractive when he was thin' and then the introductions were made.

'Charles, this is Emily Dowson, who is happily married and totally unavailable. Emily, Charles Pettison.'

They shook hands, chatted for a few moments while

Pettison drank two more sherries, then entered the restaurant, sitting at a table by the window. Within a few minutes, even before the arrival of the Soup of the Day, Emily wanted to get up and leave and return to Dowson. She could think of no reason to stay any longer away from him; the conversation she would have once enjoyed seemed petty and dull to her (anecdotes about parties, about Bindel the poet who marches in the morning to ban Capital Punishment and plots in the evening to shoot the Bourgeoisie, the whole London and county merry-go-round), and if it had been her own car outside, not Martha's, she would have left. Emily even contemplated feigning an illness, but then anticipated the well-meaning but cloying fuss that would be made by friends and waiters, and so abandoned the idea. She would endure the meal, almost with a sense of smug satisfaction as she thought constantly about Dowson, wondering what he was doing, resolving in her mind that no matter what happened, she would do everything to make him happy.

It was obvious therefore that she could not resist talking about him, and she did, telling them about the excursions she and Christopher had made to various parts of Wiltshire (even taking the place of Victoria at Stourhead) and of the presents he had brought from Rome and Florence. It was while she was talking about Florence, that she became aware of Pettison staring at her across the table, a look of puzzlement on his face until he finally said:

'Dowson! Of course ... '

Everyone stopped and looked at him.

'Dowson,' he repeated, then to Emily: 'When *was* he in Florence?'

'Christopher? Let me see. It must have been last summer. June or July. Why?'

Pettison's face reddened even more as if aware that he had impulsively entered something he shouldn't have started and so attempted to dismiss the conversation. Emily however repeated the question, smiling:

'Why did you ask that?'

'Oh, nothing ... '

Emily looked at him:

'There must have been some reason.'

Immediately Martha attempted to interrupt but Emily, who by now had sealed her dislike of Pettison, was insistent.

'It's all right,' she said. 'You can say whatever you like. He wasn't with me then. In fact, we hardly knew each other. I'm just curious. Did you meet Christopher there?'

'Well ... I don't know about Christopher,' Pettison said, as Rupert and Martha stared fixedly at their plates. 'I never knew his first name. We stayed in the same hotel and they put me and someone called Dowson at the same table. I suppose because we were both English.'

'Oh, I see,' Emily said. 'Well, then why are you so secretive about it?'

'I wasn't—' Pettison began.

'I was still Mrs Hallam then. Still married to my first husband. I'm just fascinated to know what happened.'

'Nothing happened,' Pettison replied. 'We just chatted about England and things like that. Then when his aunt arrived, he left.'

There was a momentary silence and Rupert attempted to signal to the waiter.

'His aunt?' Emily asked quietly.

'Yes ... That's what he said. I thought it might have been his mother—'

'She's dead,' said Emily.

'I know. He told me.'

'What was this woman like? His aunt.'

Pettison glanced around helplessly, then shrugged:

'I can't really say. I only glimpsed her in the corridor. About fifty, I suppose. Very well dressed.'

'Was she English?'

'I don't think so. She looked Italian, but it was difficult to see. Look, I don't even know whether it *was* your husband. I've never met him. All I know was that the man in Florence was called Dowson.'

Immediately, Emily opened her handbag. Rupert and Martha stared at each other in embarrassment as a photograph was placed before Pettison.

'Was this him?' Emily asked, her voice steady.

Pettison studied the picture for a moment, then shook his head and handed the photograph back.

'No. Nothing like him. The Dowson I'm talking about was blond.'

*　　*　　*

After lunch, Emily and Martha went shopping as planned, leaving Pettison and Rupert in the bar till they returned. They ordered brandy and moved to the empty stone fireplace, leaning against the mantel beside a row of horse-brasses.

'Listen,' Rupert said immediately, 'you're a bloody idiot telling that story about Dowson and his aunt.'

'I didn't mean to,' Pettison protested, 'it just happened. Anyway, she insisted.'

'Well, it's lucky it *wasn't* her husband.'

'But it was.'

Rupert stopped drinking and turned and looked at the other man, stunned:

'What! But you said—'

'I know what I said. I lied. I had to.'

Rupert closed his eyes in despair:

'Well, I damn well hope she believes you.'

'I'm sorry. But I'm sure she believed it was someone else. I saw it in her face.'

Rupert glanced suddenly at the door as someone entered but it was a stranger.

'Well, anyway,' he said finally, 'I suppose it *could* have been his aunt.'

There was no answer. He looked at Pettison who was staring at the ground.

'*Couldn't* it?'

'When I saw them in the corridor,' Pettison said, 'she was giving him money and touching him and trying to hold him. But as soon as he got the money he walked away.'

'You mean he was pimping?'

'Yes,' Pettison sighed. 'What else?'

Emily collected her car from Stadshunt and drove back while it was still light. On the seat next to her were two dresses she had bought, a fresh supply of make-up, a set of Carmen rollers (present from Martha), gifts for the children and a leather-bound copy of *The Natural History of Selbourne* for Dowson. She drove well and fast — a skill she was proud of — eager to see her husband, images of him in the garden, or fishing with Thomas for perch, both of them sitting in their favourite spot beneath a willow.

When she arrived home, she could hear the television in the playroom, and looked in to see the three youngest children, faces fixed in the direction of the screen, glancing up only to receive the presents and a kiss from their mother.

'Where's Victoria?'

'Outside. With Christopher.'

Emily left and wondered whether she ought to put on one of the new dresses, but she was nervous for they were different, and more fashionable than what she usually wore, and so decided to wait till later that evening. She therefore went immediately into the garden, the book in its gift-wrapping in her hand and saw Dowson on the bench, a sketch-pad on his lap, drawing the side of the house.

As she approached, he looked up and smiled immediately and Emily hurried to him and hugged him.

'I've missed you,' he said, kissing her on the cheek.

'Missed you too,' and the book was placed in his hand. 'Present.'

'For me? What is it?'

'Surprise.'

Dowson grinned then began to undo the wrapping-paper.

'Victoria's got a surprise as well. A new dress.'

'A new dress for herself?' Emily asked.

Dowson nodded and gestured across towards the elm-tree.

'You can see,' he said, 'she's wearing it now. I had a woman in the village make it up from an old dress of yours.'

Emily turned and looked across the lawn. Victoria was standing quite still, staring, not at her but at Dowson. The dress she was wearing was sleeveless and made of cotton, with a pattern of fuchsias on a field of watchet blue.

Sixteen

It had begun slowly, as a mere gesture to the dead man. A hand-out to the public's nostalgia. An early classic had been re-released in the West End of London in October 1968 and to the surprise of the management had drawn queues for four weeks, so that a limited run was extended indefinitely. Consequently, eager to show the world that they had a heart of gold (or, at least, were prepared to invest in one), the studios began to take other films from the shelves and by January 1969, cinemas in New York, London and Los Angeles were showing six of Leith's more famous successes in rotation.

Two biographies were published in six months (feign-and-punch prose dwelling on the sensational) and journalists and critics who had once dismissed the actor as a puppet in doublet and hose now clamoured to write thoughtful tributes for the intellectual press, passing the *Thesaurus* from one to the other as they sought meaningful adjectives. Each frame of *Robin Hood* and *Elizabeth and Leicester* was dusted and analysed with the devotion of an archaeologist, essays were written by the score, and certain reviewers even discovered that it was possible to write more than a paragraph on a film that was neither black-and-white nor sub-titled. Leith's face appeared everywhere, and by spring, the youth of Europe and America had adopted him as a hero, treating him either as a Victim of Capitalist Exploitation or as a randy fucker, depending on which magazine one read. Anecdotes (mostly false) were repeated incessantly, people who weren't his friends claimed to be, his fourth wife appeared in black by Balmain and that multi-lingual hybrid, the *cinéaste*, was actually seen in the daylight, resenting the cult because it was too popular, and wearing the expression of someone who has just heard an errand boy whistling his favourite esoteric piece by Pergolesi.

Naturally Dowson, even in his rural hermitage, was aware of these events, but he treated them with the disdain they deserved. The memory of those wretched months in Rome and then of the cremation itself could not be forgotten. In March, when it was discovered that Leith had spent the last weeks of his life with him, two national newspapers (and one quarterly) approached him to write his reminiscences of the actor, but Dowson ignored them. By August, however, on the first anniversary of Leith's death, the cheque-book homage had entered its peak. A retrospective exhibition of a dozen of Leith's films, beginning with *The Valley Of Death* (1936; Dir., Michael Curtiz) was announced by the National Film Theatre and an official biography, authorized by the widow, appeared in the left-hand window of Hatchard's and on the centre table at Doubleday's.

These events, however, were eclipsed by the most colourful highlight of the proceedings: a Memorial Service in St Martin-in-the-Fields, followed by a buffet/party ('as Leith would have liked us all to remember him') at the Dorchester Hotel. Tickets were by invitation only, except for those living in Islington and Kensington who found an excuse to attend these things anyway. One of the tickets was addressed to Mr and Mrs Christopher Dowson and, to everyone's surprise, it was accepted.

Although the invitation included both husband and wife, it was only Dowson himself who eventually went to London. It is certain that Emily was never persuaded to remain in Wiltshire, though she originally anticipated that Dowson would want her to accompany him, as is suggested in a letter written on August 18th:

Christopher and I were at first reluctant to accept the invitation but now it seems that he is lying in the gutter once more, surrounded by strangers who are peering at him, and that this time we ought to be there.

However, despite this feeling of guilt, Emily wasn't there, grateful that Dowson did not insist that they journey together. She convinced herself that she had to look after the children (although alternative arrangements could have been made) and so remained, the secure dormouse in the teapot, mirror in darkness.

'I couldn't face all those people,' Emily told Dowson. 'Not any more. Besides, as you once said, if I go with you, you can't return to me and I *want* you to do that.'

Dowson smiled and said that it would only be for two days and he would be back before the weekend.

'I need to go,' he added. 'When I see what the vultures are doing to Leith, I need to make at least one gesture of friendship. The man is dead and whatever they do now, they cannot destroy my feelings for him.'

Dowson repeated this remark to me in London when I showed my surprise that he had emerged from his shell, and I believed that that was the sole reason for his decision. What I didn't know then was that he had received a second letter, marked *Personal*, from the Dorchester Hotel itself, the contents of which he revealed neither to Emily nor myself. It was after this that he finally decided to go to London, though with a nervous reluctance, as if about to confront a reality that he had been hiding from us all. As it happened, it was exactly that, and on August 29th, he packed some clothes in preparation for taking the afternoon train from Pewsey.

'After all,' he repeated to Emily, placing a dinner jacket in a suitcase, 'it *is* only for a couple of days. I'll be back on Saturday morning.'

'And when you return, it'll be a wonderful weekend. I know it will.'

186

She then moved to kiss him, but Dowson appeared not to notice the action and picked up the case and left the room.

The children were waiting outside the house and Dowson stopped and looked at them, studying each one in turn, before smiling and moving to a taxi that had been hired. Behind him, Emily appeared at the door as he placed the case in the car and looked at the house:

'Those flowers should be out when I return,' he said, casually pointing to a wall of yellow buds.

'The oriental clematis?'

'Yes.'

Dowson smiled and said goodbye to the children and was about to enter the taxi when Victoria ran up to him and hugged him. Emily watched as Dowson kissed her daughter on the cheek and said something she couldn't hear, then the taxi door was closed. As the car reversed into the road, Emily turned slowly back into the house. She heard Victoria shout to Dowson:

'Can we have a special-special game when you come back?' then the taxi drove away.

That evening, Emily took the photograph albums from the cupboard and locked the drawing-room door. She lit a fire in the grate and slowly burnt every picture of herself that had been taken since the age of eleven. The process took almost one hour.

*   *   *

At first, I was convinced that he had taken another train. He had asked me to meet him and yet as I waited at the station-barrier, watching the people emerging from the carriages, there seemed no sign of him. Red-faced holiday-makers from the West Country with pottery ballast in their suitcases pushed past me, and as I glanced anxiously from one to the other as they moved along the platform, it seemed as if half of England was descending on London, and yet Dowson was nowhere to be seen. Eventually the platform was empty, and the gates beside me were being opened to allow departing passengers to move in and take the place of the arrivals. Dowson, it was apparent, had either missed the train or had decided at the last moment not to come at all. In a way, I had feared that might happen, having no reliance on him whatsoever, and was about to turn away when I saw him. He was emerging slowly from a first-class carriage, his actions hesitant as he took out his suitcase and a coat, then he turned towards the barrier, fifty yards away, just as the queues next to me surged towards him. For a moment, he appeared to retreat (a hand reaching back towards the door) then he moved aside and began to walk towards me, not seeing me, but in my direction.

Although it had been only two months since we had last met, there was no doubt that he had changed. He was still handsome, still the frontispiece for *Childe Harold*, his blue eyes and dark hair contrasting with the pallid faces around him, and yet that self-assurance that had always irritated others appeared less evident, even from this distance, and he looked almost vulnerable. Making no attempt to attract his attention I watched him as he made his way along the edge of the platform, obscured for a moment by heads, a porter driving a string of mail-trolleys, then reappearing closer, glancing nervously from one person to another, jostled by the crowds.

Then suddenly, an incident occurred, not in any way dramatic, but an incident nevertheless. Dowson was about twenty yards away from me when a man about his own age came out of the crowd and approached him. By the manner of the action, seemingly amicable, and the expression on the man's face, it was obvious that he recognized Dowson, and in fact, though I couldn't hear what was said, there was no doubt Dowson himself was startled by the encounter. The stranger, who appeared to be English (strawberry-leaf good looks and City suit) attempted to shake hands, but was ignored. He then tried to pursue Dowson once more, but was pushed aside as if he were a tout. At this moment, I myself was seen and although I glanced away, pretending I had not noticed anything, it was clear I had been a witness. Unable to resist my curiosity, I turned back just as Dowson reached me and looked past him towards the other man, who was standing, a look of hurt puzzlement on his face, then he called out a name. I couldn't quite understand it, but whatever it was, Dowson made no reaction and walked through the barrier, acknowledging me with a brief nod.

I caught up with him, hoping for an explanation and was told, without asking:

'He thought he knew me. But it was a mistake.'

'Oh, I see,' I said, not looking at him, then pointed toward the Rolls.

'The car's over there.'

We approached it in silence, until I asked:

'Emily—how is she?'

'She's well.'

'Good. I'm sorry she couldn't be here.'

Dowson looked at me, his face emotionless, then handed his suitcase to Denbigh. The car door was opened, and as he entered I noticed that he glanced quickly back towards the platform, but the stranger, whoever he was, had gone.

'Does it often happen?' I said, as we drove out of the station.

'What?'

'That you are mistaken for someone else?'

There was a pause as Dowson lit a cigarette and stared out at the hospital and shops of Paddington.

'Sometimes,' he answered finally, then added almost to himself: 'I suppose I must expect that.'

I thought of the stories of Biarritz and Florence (gossip,

of course, being in season) and wondered if it could all be the coincidence of mistaken identity. For Emily's sake I hoped it was, but I myself believed differently, and until Dowson himself proved otherwise, I was prepared to believe every gutter scandal I heard. Within twenty-four hours, however, the truth about the man sitting next to me was revealed, and I learnt that Abel-Hardy, Pettison and the stranger at the station had made no mistake whatsoever.

*   *   *

The Memorial Service the following morning was a farce. Even in the dignity of St Martin-in-the-Fields, the congregation behaved like mindless gawpers at the premiere of a musical, swivelling their heads constantly to the rear of the church as each guest arrived, then looking away with disappointment if the person was neither a celebrity, St Martin himself nor a topless nun. They sat through the sermons and the hymns as if they were irritating travelogues before the main feature, checking their watches in case they were late for lunch at the Tiberio or Isow's. Those on the left-hand side of the aisle (family, relations and pets) gaped at those on the right-hand side (studio, starlets and yawns) and vice-versa, and were silent only when a leading actor accepted the role (basic fee plus make-up) of delivering the eulogy from the pulpit. All stood up for the finale and sang the theme music from one of Leith's films and then hurried out to pose on the steps for the photographers. As Dowson observed, if there was any consolation in Leith being dead, it was that he could neither witness the travesty nor be sent the bill.

When Dowson finally returned to my apartment in Hyde Park Gate (where he was staying while Antony Bowness was in Emily's flat) it was early evening. I myself was in the study overlooking the street and the park and wasn't aware of his arrival until I went towards the drawing-room to pour myself a whisky and saw his coat and the Memorial programme on the chair. I called out his name, but there was no answer, then I found him sitting in his bedroom, in the half-light of the evening, sitting in a chair as if he were asleep. I turned to leave when he said quietly:

'Don't go.'

I hesitated, more out of surprise than anything else, for there was something in Dowson's manner that was unnerving. In the year that I had known him, he had never implied that he needed anyone (apart from Emily), least of all myself. And yet there was a feeling of need here, even if it was simply a request for me to stay.

'All right ... but may I get you a drink?'

'No, thank you.'

I nodded and closed the door and sat on the edge of the bed. I could hear the telephone ringing, considered answering it but didn't move. It seemed to ring for an eternity and then finally it stopped and there was silence.

'Where is the party tonight?' Dowson asked.

'Surely you don't want to go there now—after this morning?'

There was no answer, so I said:

'The Dorchester.'

'Oh yes ... ' Dowson replied, as if he knew all the time.

'We can go late and leave early.'

Dowson looked up, considering this, then said:

'I want you to stay the weekend with us. Go back with me tomorrow.'

'Well, I—What about Emily? She might not want me—'

'I'll tell her. *Will* you?'

'There are one or two things I have to do first—'

'Please. I need to talk to you.'

The telephone suddenly rang again. The same caller, perhaps, believing he or she had dialled wrongly the first time. I looked at Dowson, his face now almost in shadow, and said:

'All right. I'd like to very much.'

There was no reaction and I believed there was nothing more he wanted to say. I therefore stood up, on the excuse that I ought to answer the phone and walked to the door. As I opened it, he said in a low voice, so low that I had to close the door again in order to hear:

'That man at the station yesterday ... He used to be the Victor Ludorum at my old school. He hasn't changed at all. After all these years, he just hasn't changed at all ... '

I didn't say anything, but merely opened the door again and walked quietly into the next room in order to answer the telephone, but by the time I got there, the caller had rung off.

*   *   *

Emily made no attempt to telephone again that evening. Instead, she returned to her bedroom and sat looking at the mahogany box she had taken from Dowson's cupboard. For a long time she didn't try to open it, though the key was in her hand, but merely touched the polished wood, tracing the inlay of brass with her finger, her hand constantly returning to the lock itself. Finally, the key was inserted, the lid raised and the contents were revealed.

Apprehensively, Emily placed them one by one on the desk: four red-covered exercise books, written in long-hand in the form of a journal, some photographs, a collection of postcards of England, letters, a white ticket to Keats's room in Rome, two for the *Moreska*, an anthology of English poetry, a yellowed clipping from a Greek newspaper and a crumpled cigarette packet with the words ΜΠΑΥΡΟΝ ΠΑΠΑΣΤΡΑΤΟΣ on the cover. Nothing else. The first exercise book was opened (the same that Leith had read in Rome) and as Emily was half-way through it, she stopped in cold realization and looked quickly through the photographs till she found one of a girl with blonde hair, staring into the camera, smiling. Suddenly, Emily looked around startled as she heard someone enter the room and saw Victoria, standing near her in the blue dress.

'What do you want?' Emily said quickly. 'Why didn't you knock on the door?'

'I *did* knock on the door.'

'I never heard you.'

'I knocked twice,' Victoria insisted.

'Well, what do you want?'

'I just wanted to say good night.'

Emily looked at her, then smiled apologetically and took her daughter's hand.

'I'm sorry ... '

Victoria leant forward to kiss her mother, then saw the photograph on the desk:

'Who's that woman, Mama?'

'Her name's Celia.'

'Is she a friend of yours?'

'She was, but she's dead now.'

'Just like our tree,' Victoria said, turning away.

Emily stared at her, puzzled:

'What tree?'

'Oh, there's a marvellous tree on Mrs Fitzherbert that's dead. Christopher said it was probably struck by lightning. It's our favourite tree because its beautiful and preserved and Christopher calls it Celia. He said that unlike all the other trees, it would never change now. Because it's dead.'

'And he calls it Celia?'

'Yes. Good night.'

Victoria then kissed Emily and walked to the door, glancing back to see her mother slowly placing the objects on the desk back into the box, placing them carefully as if they were as fragile as porcelain.

*   *   *

'Is it true that he used to call everyone "Old Beaver"?'

'No. "Old Sport".'

'How fascinating. Absolutely fascinating.'

We are at the Dorchester (ballroom black-tie, old favourites from the bandstand) sitting at one of the tables surrounding the dance floor. The conversation is trivial, actors erecting roof-tops to shout from, and the champagne is warm. I am bored and so is Dowson sitting next to me and drinking heavily, answering the barrage of inane questions from earnest middle-aged critics with a casual tolerance that is admirable in the circumstances. The orchestra lowers another standard ('Stardust') and I turn towards my neighbour:

'Christopher — are you sure you want to stay? We've been here two hours.'

'I must.'

'But you don't owe these people anything. Look at them. I'm sure even Leith would have escaped by now.'

'I must stay,' Dowson repeated and poured himself another drink. I stared at him, puzzled by his behaviour. I can understand his drinking (affairs like this would drive Moses to the gin), but he appeared anxious, glancing at the door or at his watch, as if expecting someone to arrive. Or more accurately, as if hoping someone would not.

'Then I'm going to dance,' I said. 'There are at least two women here worthy of my attention. Both married of course, but then beautiful women usually are. If you want me, I'll be at Abel-Hardy's table.'

'Is *he* here?'

'Abel-Hardy, like God, is everywhere. But unlike God, he usually has the pick of the Season in tow.'

I stood up, hesitated, then added:

'Oh — and by the way, Emily's husband is here as well.'

Dowson looked up at me and I realized immediately what I had said:

194

'I'm sorry,' I continued quickly, 'I meant her first husband. Hallam.'

There was a smile and Dowson said:

'I know what you meant. I was just wondering whether
you were telling me or warning me. I assure you I am not in
the mood for duels.'

He then turned away as someone inquired once again
about Leith's private measurements.

From that moment on, the party was endured with
stoicism. I listened to speeches from the inarticulate, suffered
the arrogance of directors who took sole credit if their
wretched film was a success and blamed the producers if it
wasn't, and observed that delightful feminine achievement,
the bottom, with overt pleasure. Abel-Hardy himself preferred breasts (*very* un-English) and especially those of a
blackjack dealer from the neighbouring Playboy Club:

'They're amazing. Both of them. Don't you think they're
amazing?'

I agreed that they were amazing since they were competing on the table with the condiments, but they were far
from being aesthetic. Breasts, as far as I am concerned,
should be polite, have preferably one nipple each and be no
larger than the Harrods grapefruit I eat when I'm on a diet.
Abel-Hardy then table-hopped, someone sang about a
cigarette with lipstick traces, and then at eleven-thirty I
realized that Dowson was no longer in the room.

Thinking at first that he might be ill, I inquired at his
table, but received evasive answers, shrugs, and was finally
told that he had been seen moving towards the hotel foyer·

'But did he seem all right?'

'A bit drunk. That's all.'

'Was he alone?'

'Yes.'

Immediately, I made my way across the dance-floor, pushing through couples (feverish assignations as the last waltz

reached its reprise) and approached the corridor that led to the entrance. Ahead of me I could see Abel-Hardy again, inevitably, but this time praising the intelligence of an actress who specialized (at least in public) as a nude vampire. Respecting this overture to an amourette, I attempted to pass them both by discreetly. However, I was seen and Abel-Hardy hurried towards me, drawing me aside like a conspirator:

'It's the same woman,' he blurted out, glancing furtively around.

'Is she? Congratulations.'

'Not her! With Dowson. It's the same bloody woman.'

'What are you talking about?'

'*Dowson*. He was in the lobby with the same woman I saw in Biarritz.'

I stared at him, stared at his gaping face, trying to rationalize what he had just said. Behind him, the vampire flew away.

'Are you sure?'

'Of course I'm damn well sure.'

'The same woman—'

'The same bloody woman who was in Biarritz.'

I believed him. Abel-Hardy does not need to lie nor does he make mistakes.

'*When* did you see Dowson?'

'About twenty minutes ago. He talked to her for a while, then she took his arm and they went upstairs in the lift.'

Oh hell, I thought, *why* does he still do it? I could accept it when it was in the past, but not now, before everyone, now that he's married to Emily.

'Hallam saw them too,' Abel-Hardy added, turning the knife.

'What!'

'He saw them. He was with me and he saw them.'

196

'For Godsakes, doesn't Dowson bloody well *care*?'

'Hallam does. He said he was going to phone Emily and tell her.'

'Well, I hope you stopped him.'

Abel-Hardy shrugged, a look of satisfaction on his face: 'Why should I?' he said.

'Because Emily's not Hallam's wife any more. I know he's drunk and jealous, but it's still none of his business.'

'The children are.'

I looked at Abel-Hardy, hating him, but realizing that I might well have done the same thing in his place. My tolerance for Dowson was rapidly coming to an end and I believe I was glad of it. My thoughts now were concerned solely for Emily, and in truth, they always have been.

'We've got to telephone her,' I said, moving towards a booth in the corner.

'What the hell for?'

'Because we don't know what Hallam might have said to her.'

'Well, Dowson deserves it, doesn't he?'

'What makes you so damn pious?' I said angrily and didn't wait for an answer, for I was already talking to the operator, giving her the number. It was, of course, engaged. Fearing the worst, I asked for the signal to be checked and was told, after what seemed like an eternity, that in fact there was no conversation. Emily had apparently taken the telephone off the hook.

'She often does that,' I said, trying to convince myself. 'When she wanted an early night, she often used to do that. She probably did it before Hallam phoned.'

There was a look of scepticism from Abel-Hardy and I can't say I blamed him. Nevertheless, there was still the possibility, meagre as it was, that I was right, though I could only be sure when I found Hallam himself and asked him. I therefore moved across the corridor, past the entrance to the lobby and it was then that I saw them both, standing in the left-hand corner by the doors.

'Is that the same woman?' I asked.

Abel-Hardy looked, then nodded:

'Yes. It's the same woman.'

She was standing facing me, looking up at Dowson, one hand on his arm. At this distance she looked any age between forty and fifty years old, very attractive and dressed in superb taste. Dark hair and eyes, slim, the type of woman one expects to see winning in *la salle privée* or dining at Maxim's. An international face, Latin by blood, one would think, and with a natural style of movement that could only have been passed down from grandparent to parent. As has already been said, I have seen many women of varying nationalities who infest the world of leisure and grand hotels, and yet I had never encountered this particular woman before. Certainly she could have belonged to that set with ease, and yet she seemed far removed from it, solitary, a trace of nervous sadness as she talked to Dowson. There was one thing that was very clear. She did not seem the type to pick up gigolos, even if they were as attractive as Christopher Dowson himself.

'What I don't understand,' I asked Abel-Hardy, 'is why it should be the *same* woman?'

'God knows. Maybe she just pays more.'

'I'm going over there,' I said.

'You can't—' Abel-Hardy began, startled, but I was already crossing the carpet towards the door. I make no apologies for my behaviour in encroaching on what was evidently a private conversation and no affair of mine whatsoever. I could attribute my action to the champagne, or my natural impulse, but that is not so. I was sick of the enigma and wanted the truth, even if I had to be brazen and meddlesome to find it out.

'Ah, there you are, Christopher,' I said with a stage-managed smile, not looking at the woman. 'I was wondering where you were.'

There was a momentary pause as the woman glanced at me (exquisite eyes, a mouth by Renoir), then Dowson turned, after lighting a cigarette, and said quite casually:

'You're beginning to behave like a Nanny.'

'I'm sorry ... I didn't realize you were with someone.'

'Didn't you? Well, now you see that I am.'

It was a foolish mistake and I was regretting my action, when Dowson gestured to the woman and said to me:

'Perhaps now you are here, you would like to meet Mrs Tzavelas.'

The tone in his voice seemed to imply a proposition, as if he had misinterpreted my intentions, but the woman appeared unconcerned and politely extended her hand and I was introduced. There was then a silence as Dowson made no attempt to say anything, but simply looked at me, a slight flicker of amusement on his face.

'Tzavelas?' I said, desperately trying to think of an exit line. 'Is that Spanish or Greek?'

'Greek,' the woman replied (a slight accent) turning back towards Dowson.

'Ah yes. And are you here on holiday?'

The woman didn't reply, her hand moving to her neck in a self-conscious gesture, then she murmured: 'Excuse me,' and moved quickly away to stand by the desk, glancing back in our direction.

'I'm sorry,' I said to Dowson. 'I didn't mean to be impertinent, intruding like that.'

He looked at me, then across the lobby to where Abel-Hardy was watching, then nodded as if he had heard everything Abel-Hardy had told me and understood exactly my motives.

'I am not a fool,' he said. 'I am quite aware what everybody has been saying. And they are right. It *is* the same woman who was in Biarritz and Florence and other places too. She gives me money.'

'Look, Christopher,' I began, unable to control my embarrassment, 'whatever you do is your business. I won't say a word to Emily—'

Dowson suddenly startled me by laughing and said:

'But why not? The woman is a relation.'

'Of course,' I replied, seeking to vindicate myself. 'She's your aunt.'

Dowson looked at me suddenly in surprise:

'My aunt? Whatever made you think she was my aunt?'

'Well, Pettison said—'

'Whoever Pettison is, he's wrong. Mrs Tzavelas is not my aunt. She's my mother.'

He then carefully stubbed out his cigarette in an ashtray by the door and walked past me, moving, without looking back, out of the hotel, abandoning the woman at the desk. I looked at her and whoever she was, she appeared now helpless and isolated, an anonymous woman drifting from city to city and from hotel to hotel, living alone in a first-floor room.

Seventeen

Of course, no one was prepared to believe Dowson. If it was accepted that a woman calling herself Mrs Tzavelas was his mother, then why had he informed everyone, including Emily, that she was dead and buried on an island in Greece? To be honest, I myself no longer cared either way, and when I returned to my apartment and found that Dowson had not come back, I wasn't disappointed. I merely attempted to telephone Emily once more, without success, and then went to bed, hoping that I would never see him again. At four o'clock in the morning, however, the light in my room was turned on and he stood at the door, still dressed as he was at the party, his hair and coat wet with rain as if he had been walking. My first reaction, at this sudden awakening, was to tell him to get out, to apologize, switch off the bloody light and leave. But instead, he sat down in a chair, hunched up in profile, the same expression on his face that I had first seen at Stadshunt nearly two years before. An expression, not quite of sadness, but of regret.

'Whatever you're going to tell me,' I said irritably, 'I'd prefer it if you waited till the morning. I'm not in a very tolerant mood at this hour.'

There was a silence, then he turned and looked at me across the room, his face pale:

'I'm sorry,' he replied quietly. 'I didn't realize it was so late.'

'*Early*,' I emphasized. 'Not late. It's very early and I'm tired.'

'Perhaps if I could make you some coffee —'

'No. I don't want anything. Just go to bed.'

A pause, then Dowson stood up and walked to the door.

'I'm sorry,' he repeated, then switched off the light. I could hear him walking, not to his room, but to the kitchen, and then the sound of a kettle being filled and cupboards opened. I listened for a few more moments and then thankfully fell asleep.

When I awoke again, at the humane hour of eight o'clock, Dowson was still in the kitchen, still dressed, but sitting at the table writing in an exercise book.

'Don't tell me you've been here all the time?'

'I wasn't tired,' he replied, closing the book.

'Well, if I may say so, you look like hell.'

'I believe you.'

I hesitated, trying to think of something to say. His appearance, indeed his very attitude, disturbed me. Not that he looked ill, though he may have been, but because he seemed changed, nervous, like someone who sensed he had no right to be there. An uninvited guest who had outstayed his welcome and I felt that at any moment he would wash up the cup and saucer and apologize for using the coffee. This impression may well have been calculated on his part, for I have seen him change his mood within a minute, often with the merest gesture or look, in order to achieve the effect he desired. Nevertheless, I found myself regretting my bad temper four hours earlier, though I certainly was not going to admit it.

'Have you had breakfast?' I asked.

'No. I'm not hungry.'

'There are some cereals somewhere —'

'No.'

Then he looked up at me and smiled:

'All right. Thank you.'

During breakfast (never my favourite meal, except in

France) Dowson finally began to talk, hesitantly at first, then more openly as he relaxed and discovered that I was not an unwilling or even an unsympathetic listener. Much of what he said I have already written (Korčula, Rome, Emily) and though I found it interesting and often revealing, I still awaited an explanation regarding the mysterious Mrs Tzavelas. Dowson obviously realized this but he took his time, as if he had to place the events in their correct order for me to understand, though the events themselves were more retrospective than progressive. For example, his child-hood (the years in Yorkshire) appeared after his meeting with Emily, while the experiences in Rome prefaced the death of his father twenty years before, and by that time he had been talking for an hour and I was almost out of cigarettes.

'When my father died, I was at school. It was during a Geography class and the headmaster came in and we stood up and he talked to the teacher, Mr D'Arcy, and they looked at me and I was called out. I thought I had done something wrong, for that wasn't unusual, but the headmaster took me to his study and asked me if I would like to sit down and then he told me that my father had died. He was very polite about it and sympathetic and asked the matron to order a car to take me to the station. It was a Humber, I believe, though I can't be sure. A Humber or a Ford. My mother wasn't at the funeral, and it wasn't until two years later that I learnt that she had married again. If she had written to me perhaps I would have understood. But she never did. I could never forgive that and I still don't. I didn't see her again till we met, by chance, in Biarritz. Her second husband had divorced her and she was alone and wanted me back. But it was too late … She pestered me, of course, gave me money, but I couldn't make her understand that I didn't want to see her. She was different and I felt nothing for her at all. In my mind she no longer existed and it was only when she threatened to go to Wiltshire that I agreed to talk to her last night. But it was a mistake … '

'Why did she leave your father?' I asked tentatively.

'She said that she didn't leave. That she ran away. Back to Greece.'

'Just like that?'

'That's what I said. "Just like that?" '

'And what did she say?'

'That if she hadn't left my father when she did, he would have left her. In time. As she grew older … '

There was a pause, then Dowson shrugged and looked away, avoiding my eye. There was a sudden sense of embarrassment and so I stood up and suggested some more coffee but it was declined.

'So Tzavelas was your mother's second husband?' I asked.

'Yes. I told you that.'

'Christopher, you also told everyone that your mother was dead.'

'The woman I knew as a child *is* dead.'

'But you know she's not. If you're telling me the truth, she's living in a hotel half a mile away.'

'But it's not the same woman. Can't you see that?'

'She's still your mother. Isn't she?'

'Not any more.'

'You hate her that much?'

'No. The years with her as a child, in the village in Yorkshire, were the happiest in my life.'

I stared at him in exasperation, found there was nothing I could say and left the room. I am neither a detective nor a psychiatrist, and frankly I am not sure I believe a word of it. Perhaps I am wrong. Perhaps you yourself are more perceptive than I and can understand that someone like Dowson could feel such an acute sense of betrayal. But my own mother left *me* when I was three and though I haven't seen her since, I certainly have never entertained the idea of

mentally killing her off to immortalize the image. To begin
with, the bitch doesn't deserve it.

'You're still coming for the weekend, aren't you?' Dowson said. He had entered the bathroom as I searched for my
electric shaver that my daily insists on tidying away. I
glanced at his face in the mirror then slowly turned and
leant on the sink, arms folded:

'Christopher ... '

'Yes?' he said innocently, as if nothing had happened.

'If what you said is true —'

'About the weekend? Of course it is. I asked you.'

'Not about the weekend,' I replied patiently. 'About your
mother.'

There was a puzzled look of someone trying to recall
exactly what I was talking about. Dowson had dismissed the
whole conversation from his mind. He had told me and as
far as he was concerned, that was that. *He's just too honest and
no one could fight that*, Antonella told me in Paris. In view of the
alternative, let us hope she is right.

'What you said about your mother,' I continued, trying
to attract his attention as he stood on the bathroom scales
and watched the revolving dial. 'I think you ought to tell
Emily.'

'Twelve stone three. I've lost two pounds.'

'Christopher — there's a chance that Hallam telephoned
her last night. I can't be sure that he did because the phone
might have been off the hook, but he saw you with your ...
with Mrs Tzavelas. Do you understand what I'm saying?'

Dowson remained studying the dial for a moment, then
looked at me:

'Yes. Yes I do.'

'Then you'll telephone Emily? Before we go?'

There was a pause, then he nodded and stepped off the
scales and walked past me towards the door. As he reached
it, he suddenly stopped and put his hand on my arm:

'My mother has invited Emily and the children to stay with her in Italy,' he said. 'Her husband has a villa in Tuscany.'

'But I thought she was divorced from him?'

'He ... left it to her. It's too big for her to live there on her own.'

'I see.'

He smiled, considered what he had said, then left. I heard the telephone ring once as it was picked up, then twenty minutes later, Dowson reappeared, dressed in casual clothes, ready to leave.

'What did she say?' I asked, as we closed the door of the apartment.

'Who?'

'Emily.'

'Oh,' Dowson replied, 'it was engaged,' and then walked to the lift, holding the doors open for me, Denbigh and the luggage. We were driving to Wiltshire, not only because it was more comfortable than by train, but also because it was quicker, all in all, and I was suddenly anxious, though I tried not to show it, about Emily.

During the journey, despite my own fears, Dowson appeared more relaxed than I had seen him for months. He sat next to me, smiling, urging Denbigh to drive faster, eager, it appeared, to return home.

'My mind is filled with plans for Emily. Perhaps we'll move to London, visit her friends. See everything we have missed.'

'I assure you,' I said, 'you have not missed much.'

'But do you realize,' Dowson said, as if suddenly aware of the fact for the first time, 'that Emily and I have hardly left the house for months?'

I didn't answer. Denbigh, a chauffeur without equal, was driving well and fast and avoiding all the congested roads, but even so there was still at least an hour before we reached our destination.

'By the way, I must thank you,' Dowson said, leaning towards me.

'For what?'

'For listening to me this morning. I hated having to lie about my mother, but now that I've told the truth, I feel much happier. I don't mind if you consider me callous, but I couldn't bear to be thought dishonest. I chose to tell you first, because I knew you, of all people, would understand.'

Dowson then smiled and put his feet up on the casual seat opposite.

'When I tell Emily later,' he added, gazing through the partition at the road ahead, 'I know that you'll be there to support me.'

I turned and stared at him in sudden realization:

'Is *that* why you invited me for the weekend?' I asked cautiously.

Dowson laughed, not answering my question, and leant forward and told Denbigh to stop at the nearest florist.

'I'll buy her flowers,' he explained, turning back towards me, 'flowers for Emily and the children. We'll fill the car with flowers.'

'It'll look like a hearse.'

Dowson glanced at me, contemplated the image, then nodded:

'Yes. Why not?'

'Then who is the corpse? As a mourner I ought to know.'

'Oh, the corpse is not a person.'

'I'm relieved to hear it. Then what exactly is dead?'

He hesitated, then looked about him in a mock parody of a conspirator:

'My England,' he replied, laughing.

'Very melodramatic.'

'Very.'

At Marlborough, we bought flowers (lilies, carnations) though only a few bunches, for that was all there was. Nevertheless, the flowers themselves seemed to be a pleasant overture to the weekend. Though I am not a superstitious man by nature, I believed that all could be well, and that whatever happened, the next two days would be more than memorable.

And they were.

Eighteen

The house was deserted. I expected to see the children, or at least hear them, but there was no sound whatsoever. Dowson and I had left Denbigh with the car at an inn in the village (*The Boar*, low beams, a tribute to Richard III) and had walked across the green, past swings and Memorial. Then, as we approached the gate, the silence seemed unnerving.

'Perhaps Emily's taken the children for a walk,' I suggested.

'Perhaps.'

I followed Dowson into the house and waited as he toured the rooms, calling out his wife's name, but there was no answer. At my feet, the morning newspaper still lay on the doormat, but then there is often a late delivery in the country. When Dowson finally reappeared I asked him if Emily had left a message.

'I couldn't see one,' he replied, unconcerned.

'On the mantelpiece or by the telephone? Those are the usual places, aren't they?'

And without waiting for an answer, I moved through the partition door into the passage by the drawing-room.

'Well,' I said, gesturing to the telephone, 'she's replaced the phone on the hook.'

'No. *I* did that just now,' replied Dowson.

'Oh, I see.'

'Yes.'

He then smiled:

'They're probably all in the garden. On a day like this, that's where they would be.'

'But they would have heard you, wouldn't they?'

Dowson shrugged:

'Let's find out.'

The garden however seemed as empty as the house and we were about to turn away ('The housekeeper Mrs Powell might know') when the welcoming committee appeared, blonde hair and blue dress, running across the lawn towards us to be picked up and hugged.

'When did you arrive?'

'Just now.'

'Good, because I thought we could all play a special-special game.'

'Of course. What game do you have in mind?'

That familiar pose of concentration (head on an angle, lower lip under upper teeth, left eye screwed up, gazing into space) then she replied:

'Flower-initials or treasure hunt?'

I smiled, joining in the mood and took her hand and said:

'It's good to see you, Emily. We wondered where you were.'

Emily squeezed my hand and answered her own question:

'I think it'll be a treasure hunt.'

*   *   *

The game was planned for the afternoon, and as it was a sunny day we decided to have lunch in the garden, the three of us sitting around a wooden table in the shadow of an elm. The lawn had just been mown and there was a smell of grass and of roses and of the warm bread Emily had baked herself. She sat opposite me looking more beautiful and happier than I can remember, fussing around us both, a straw hat with a blue ribbon on her head. All my fears had been morbid and melodramatic and I realized how easy and dangerous it was to allow one's imagination to suspect the worst of the most innocent situations. Emily had been at the end of the garden and had not heard us arrive, and the reason why the children were not there was because they had gone to spend a few days in Cumberland with their grandmother, who had collected them the night before. It was as simple as that. Looking at Emily and Dowson together now, it seemed incredible that I had ever questioned their happiness or had believed that anything sinister had taken place. Such is the destructive nature of envy and I confess I felt suddenly ashamed. I had wanted, like Abel-Hardy and the others, to doubt Dowson's integrity, to be suspicious of every action, of everything he said. And yet here I was, a guest at his house, sharing a weekend with two people who were treating me with the natural hospitality that is reserved only for a closest friend. It was a privilege I wouldn't now sacrifice for the world, and if that sounds pretentious, I make no apologies. My only regret is that I hadn't been invited to stay for a month or even longer. Next time, I think I'll insist.

'Those are Japanese anemones,' Emily said, pointing to the flowers behind us. 'The white ones. And the mauve ones are called "Prince Henry", though I'm not sure which Henry it is. I planted them two years ago and they're marvellously easy to grow, except that they don't like being moved. I haven't tried to move them but that's what she says in the book. Vita Sackville-West. Have you ever been to Sissinghurst? Oh, and those are gentians. Marvellous blue. I adore them.'

I looked at Dowson as he leant over and kissed Emily on the cheek. She took his arm and held on to him tightly.

'I love you, Christopher,' she said quietly, without embarrassment, not moving for a moment, as if wanting to remain there permanently. Then she suddenly turned away and hurried towards the house, saying that she had to prepare the clues for the treasure hunt.

'Did you ask Emily if Hallam phoned?' I said to Dowson when his wife had left.

'I don't need to. You can see for yourself that even if he had, it would make no difference between us.'

'Yes I can,' I answered, then after a moment's hesitation: 'Christopher ... I must say this. I apologize if I ever ... seemed distrustful of you.'

He looked at me in surprise, then smiled:

'But it was my own fault. I realize that. Now, however, everything will change.'

'When will you tell Emily about your mother?'

'After the treasure hunt. By the way, I hope you don't mind joining in such games.'

'Of course not. It sounds rather enjoyable.'

'It is. But it's not as easy as you think.'

'Well, if it's no more difficult than *The Times* crossword,' I replied, 'I might muddle through.'

Dowson gazed in the direction of the house, then at the garden.

'It's good to come back here. Emily and I must do that often. Leave in order to return.'

As Emily prepared the notes — the series of riddles leading to the next clue until one reaches the final prize — we were obliged to wait in the drawing-room so that we could not see the hiding-places. Dowson had put some white wine on ice and we sat, listening to Delius, and opened the first bottle. Now and again we caught glimpses of Emily through the window and made dramatic gestures of hiding our eyes as she pulled a face, giggled then hurried away.

'She's as excited about the game as a child,' I said, smiling, pouring another glass.

Dowson turned quickly and looked at me, but said nothing. The record finished and there was a silence. I watched him as he stared at a framed photograph of the children on the desk, his face in profile, a slight puzzlement.

'Where was the picture taken?' I asked casually.

'Avebury.'

'Ah, yes.'

'There used to be a photograph of Emily in the frame but she must have put it somewhere else.'

He was about to reach for some more wine when Emily herself appeared at the door, the hat in her hand.

'There! All ready.'

Dowson grinned and stood up:

'How many clues?'

'Six.'

'Difficult or easy?'

'That depends.'

'And what is the prize?' I asked.

'Oh, you mustn't ask that,' Dowson interrupted. 'That's the whole secret.'

'Here's the first clue,' Emily said and placed a piece of paper on the table, then turned to the door:

'I'll watch from the garden but I'm not going to give you any help. None at all. So there.'

We were left alone. I picked up the note and read it aloud:

'*To find number two you must stare | Where there are suits but not to wear | And knife-less cutlery | But not to eat.* God,' I said, reading it out again, 'are they all like this?'

Dowson laughed and looked at the note.

'I think we need another glass of wine.'

'*Suits you do not wear?* What other suits are there?'

'Playing cards?' Dowson suggested, opening the desk drawer.

'Could be. Where do you keep them?'

'Here. But there's no note. Besides, what on earth is knife-less cutlery?'

'Well that means forks probably—'

'Spades!' Dowson shouted.

'What?'

'Spades. The suit. Spades and forks.'

'Garden shed?'

'Garden shed.'

And so it began.

There is little more really to say. I will describe the rest of the afternoon (and of course the result of the hunt) for various reasons, but most importantly in order to set down on paper a personal souvenir of that Saturday which I knew then could never be repeated in quite the same way. And it never was. Carrying a bottle of wine, Dowson and I pursued each clue with the dedication of Theseus (though our mood was one of exhilaration rather than bad-tempered dread) following the labyrinth of Emily's notes from garden shed to rose-bush to the middle page of *Vanity Fair*. We drank, laughed, argued over clues (*Salad days without Verdi* you can work out for yourself. It took *us* half an hour) while Emily watched from the garden bench, an enigmatic smile that outrivalled Da Vinci's tubby model, or bursting into laughter, hand to mouth, as we stumbled through nettles.

By clue five, both Dowson and I were competing in earnest, no longer assisting each other as we seized each piece of paper. Five, the penultimate, brought us to the attic (a Greek pun dictating that excursion) much to my unease since spiders have never been my favourite pet. The mere thought of them makes me shiver and glance up at the ceiling, preferring to see the sword of Damocles there than one of those hideous insects. It was this phobia, therefore, that was responsible for my lack of concentration as I read the clue a mere thirty seconds after Dowson. It wasn't that difficult as it happened, but before I could decode it, he had already left, laughing and scrambling down the attic ladder. It turned out to be the children's swings in the centre of the green (*Two-way air trip on 44 yards*) and by the time I remembered that twenty-two yards equalled a chain, I had given away five minutes and the treasure, whatever it was, seemed to be lost.

As it happened, to my relief, Dowson was still on the green, sitting on one of the swings, staring at the final clue.

'Don't tell me it's worse than the others,' I said, approaching him.

'I can't make head or tail of it. It's even written atrociously. Look at it. I thought at first it was written by a child of ten.'

I leant over him and looked at the piece of paper, the words written in crayon in a mixture of block capitals, small letters and bad spelling.

'Maybe the way Emily has written it is part of the clue?' I suggested, but Dowson was more puzzled about the text itself. In correction it read: *Near the living cricket, not the insect, is the Immortal Treasure. Happy me. Not Emily now but Rosemary.*

'Who the hell is Rosemary?' I asked, sitting on the adjacent swing.

'God knows. I've never even *met* anyone called Rosemary. Have you?'

'Not offhand.'

I took the clue and read it again, ignoring the glares of three village children who had arrived and were waiting impatiently for us to leave.

'*Near the living cricket?* That couldn't be as obvious as a cricket pitch, could it?'

Dowson shook his head:

'There *is* one, but it's miles away. She would never have had time to go there.'

'Well, what's a living cricket then if it's not the bloody insect?'

Dowson frowned and then took back the clue.

'Maybe we could ask those children,' I said.

'Cheating,' Dowson replied. 'Besides, they might claim the treasure.'

'*Living cricket?* Couldn't be willow, could it? I mean they make cricket bats out of –'

But Dowson was already on his feet.

'The willow tree! Where Thomas and I go fishing.'

He began to move away.

'But what about the rest of the clue?'

'We'll work that out when we get there. Come on. We'll get another couple of bottles on the way.'

I hurried after him across the green and back into the house. Emily was no longer in the garden as Dowson took some more wine and a corkscrew and we made our way on to the bank of the river, towards a willow tree about twenty yards away. It was still hot and the air seemed still and restful. The sound of grasshoppers in the nearby field.

When we reached the tree, Dowson sat down.

'Let's have some wine first. Did you bring the glasses?'

'Forgot. Want me to go back and get them?'

'Doesn't matter.'

He handed me a bottle and then uncorked the second and we sipped the cool wine and lay back on the bank, staring at the water, and for a while we almost forgot about the treasure hunt altogether as a pleasant drowsiness took over.

'Caught a perch here last week. Well, *I* didn't catch it. Thomas did.'

'Did you eat it?'

'No. Threw it back. Probably catch it again next week,' and Dowson laughed and suddenly, as these things happen, we were both laughing, giggling over absurd remarks and I was reminded of Emily's description of Dowson in Korčula with the Italian tourists. A dark-haired man, sun-tanned, in a white shirt and cotton trousers, supremely happy, lying on the grass amid reeds, the river and the hills before us.

'Of course,' I said suddenly, 'Rosemary could be a plant.'

'Rosemary who?'

'Rosemary in the clue. *Not Emily but Rosemary.*'

Dowson shrugged apathetically, then grinned:

'Why on earth would she want to be a plant? And why rosemary of all things? Ugly herb.'

'No idea. Rosemary? *Rosemary for remembrance.*'

'I thought that was the poppy.'

'No. In the quotation.'

'Oh,' Dowson said. 'Unlike Emily, I never was any good at quotations. Where is it from?'

'*Hamlet*. Ophelia said it.'

'Did she now? Good for her.'

Dowson leant back, his head against the willow gazing up at the sky.

'If it's like this tomorrow, we'll all go for a picnic on Lily Langtry. The left breast is the finest. Right one for kite-flying, left one for picnics.'

He then smiled and looked across at me, took another drink and said with a sigh:

'Well, I suppose we'd better go and find this damn treasure. Whatever it is.'

I watched as he got up and began to saunter along the bank, away from the house, stopping only to inquire if I had given up the chase.

'Too lazy,' I replied and waved him on.

Dowson smiled in agreement, pointed suddenly to something running across a field (a rabbit, no doubt) and wandered, a little unsteadily, further away. I myself began to day-dream, staring at the reeds and the water until I noticed that Dowson was now standing still, about thirty yards along the bank, holding something shiny in his left hand. Obviously the treasure.

'Did you find it?' I called out, walking towards him.

He held up the object, but the sun was behind him, blurring my vision.

'What on earth is it?' I asked.

'A shoe.'

'A *shoe*? What kind of prize is that?'

Nevertheless, I applauded. It might not be much of a treasure but he was the winner.

'Her dress is here too,' Dowson then said, pointing to the ground. 'All her clothes.'

'Well, it's a fine day for swimming—'

But there was no answer for Dowson was already running away from me, running along the bank of the river and calling out Emily's name.

Part Four

———————————

VICTORIA

Nineteen

The house still remains as it was when I first saw it, though the garden is not at its best any more. I suppose that was inevitable, for it was neglected while legal arrangements were made to return the four Hallam children to their natural father, and by the time it was put up for auction eight months had gone by. The house, plus contents, were bought eventually by myself at an absurd price and it is where I live now. At first, I slept in the guest-room just in case Dowson returned, but now I think I'll move next door into the main bedroom. After all, I haven't seen or heard from him since he left England three weeks after Emily's death, though it was thought for a while that he was staying in a hotel in Verona, but it may well have been Vienna or even Nice.

The last time I talked to Dowson, in fact, was after the inquest when he told me that he was leaving the country. He didn't say for how long, nor did I inquire, since it seemed superfluous. Besides, no one wants to know anything about him, except Victoria (now thirteen) who visits me whenever she gets the chance. Sometimes we simply sit and talk and listen to music, but more often we take a picnic basket and go for walks on Mrs Fitzherbert. I must admit I look forward to the days she spends with me, planning them accordingly, for I realize that she is growing up and will soon be a woman. Each time, of course, she asks me when Dowson is coming back and each time I tell her that it could be any day. But I never was a very convincing liar, and though neither of us admit it, we both know that Christopher Dowson left England in October 1969 for ever, and that there is no reason to assume any more that he will ever return.

5⁰⁰   Gen 2/15 TD